Niccoli, It's Only Temporary

Sandra S. Jones

Xulon PRESS

Library of Congress Control Number: 2002114855
ISBN 1-591604-17-6

Unless otherwise indicated, Bible quotations are taken from the King James Version, World Publishing, Co., Cleveland & New York.

Illustrations by artist Ci Paluh

To order books contact:
Jonespub@juno.com

Xulon Press
10640 Main Street
Suite 204
Fairfax, VA 22030
(703) 934-4411
XulonPress.com

To order additional copies, call 1-866-909-BOOK (2665).

3/9/03

To Amy, my this book bless you as it blessed me when I wrote it. God is so good!

Sandy

For the things that are seen are temporary, but the things that are not seen are eternal.

2nd Corth. 4:18

Dedication

Dedicated to my LORD who revealed this story to me and gently nudged me with His unwavering persistence to become an author; and to my four sons, Kevin, Arlen, Kalen and Daron, who unknowingly gave me the desire to continue on through a difficult time in my life.

Acknowledgement

There is not a book published that is the sole work of the author. There are many who either spark an idea, suggest another way to express a thought or give the blessing of encouragement. I wish to acknowledge all who have helped in their own way to make this book a reality.

I want to express special acknowledgement to those who worked directly with the process; to Sandra Schoenstein for her hours of prep work and to my husband, Bob, who has been an unquestionable helpmate.

Introduction

This book is written for all people who are mentally and physically abused, for those who feel totally alone and forsaken, and those who know the depths of despair, rejection and betrayal. May each of you find *'Niccoli, It's Only Temporary'* to be a source of realization and understanding that you are never alone and can always find the strength deep within yourself to press forward; realizing that even in your darkest hour God, your comforter, is there with you. He alone can make it possible to have a peace within that can only come from a personal relationship through His son, Jesus the Christ, who also experienced the sting of abuse, rejection, betrayal and the loneliness of being misunderstood.

CHAPTER 1

The food that Penelope had prepared hours before sat cold and untouched on the roughly hewn table, a stark reminder that Niccoli had not returned home that evening. At first she and Andros, her fellow servant, had not worried about Niccoli's tardiness because they thought that perhaps she had stopped to chat with someone and had lost track of time, but when night fell and she still was not home Andros decided that something must be terribly wrong and left in search of the missing young woman.

Penelope stayed behind so that she would be there in case their charge returned, but hours had now passed and neither Andros nor Niccoli had returned. Why? What was wrong? Couldn't he find her? The unanswered questions were becoming unbearable for Penelope and time seemed to stand still, not caring that each minute carried prolonged agony for her.

"We should all be asleep in our beds at this hour," she muttered to herself. She felt her graying hair fall forward and stick to the nervous perspiration that peppered her forehead, and as she pushed it back she noticed for the first time how badly her aging hands were trembling. "I'm too old for nonsense like this," she grumbled and pressed her pudgy palms together in an effort to quiet them.

The apprehension that she felt would not allow her to remain still and her steps took her back to the window for what must have been the hundredth time. Once again she pulled back the crude curtain that covered the small opening and peered out into the night. Perhaps this time she would see Niccoli walking towards her but, to her dismay, all she saw was the bleak darkness that blanketed the city of Jerusalem. A sickening feeling began to fester in her stomach and panic edged its way into the depths of her being.

"What if something terrible has happened and we never see her again?" she questioned out loud. Her thoughts rapidly switched to Niccoli's father, Senator Cademus, who had placed Niccoli in their care for as long as she remained in Jerusalem. "What will the Senator do when he discovers that his only child is missing?" she could hardly spit out the words because of the fear that she felt. Her knees grew weak and a shudder passed over her body.

It had been the summer of 32 AD, only four months prior, that Senator Cornelius Cademus had reluctantly permitted his daughter, Niccoli, to travel to Jerusalem. The only reason he had given in to Niccoli's insistence was with the stipulation that Penelope and Andros, his most trusted servants, would accompany her and constantly stay by her side during the time she would remain in Jerusalem. Penelope fully understood the responsibility that had been placed upon her and she had no trouble visualizing in her mind the anger that would rise up against them when the Roman Senator realized Niccoli was missing.

Tears streamed down her cheeks and she blindly groped for a chair to sit in before her legs gave way beneath her. The room began to stifle her like a tomb. The lamp, almost out of oil from burning so late into the night, started to flicker but she brushed it off as unimportant. Why should she care? She was as good as dead anyway! The senator would see to that.

Suddenly the quiet of the room was shattered by the thud of the heavy wooden door as it opened and slammed shut. Penelope, startled by the noise, quickly turned her head towards the sound and in the dim light she saw the tall silhouette of Andros standing at the door. She jumped to her feet and rushed to his side hoping that she would see Niccoli standing behind him, but to her disappointment the space behind Andros was void. Niccoli was not with him.

"Oh, please tell me you found her," she begged, and when Andros did not answer she continued, "Niccoli is safe, isn't she?" She searched for some sign of reassurance, but the look on his face needed no explanation as to the results of his search. It told her the bleak story without him saying a word. The final realization of the seriousness of the situation made her feel as though someone had taken a sharp knife and ripped her body open. She doubled over in pain and as she held her abdomen she could feel the knot that had tightened in her stomach. "What are we going to do!" she wept despairingly.

Andros watched as Penelope crumpled to the floor into a sobbing mass of hopelessness. Not being able to give her any semblance of hope, he did not know what to do or say. "I have searched everywhere," he finally replied and the strain of the evening's event reflected heavily in his voice. "I even went back to the school and awakened Mary, but she had not seen her since twilight. I just can't understand what has happened! It is as though she has vanished into thin air!"

Andros was a tall ruggedly built man but in his despair his shoulders slumped forward making him look shorter and much older than his forty-two years. Never in his life had he felt so inadequate as he did at this very moment. He wished that he could do more, but what more could he do? He already had searched the area thoroughly. Where else could he look?

His mind turned to the cloak that he had rolled into a ball

and tucked under his arm. He had found it in one of the deserted alleys that he had searched and needed for Penelope to verify if it was indeed Niccoli's. He knew that she had not yet noticed the garment and dreaded bringing it to her attention. Finally, after long hesitation, he heaved a heavy sigh and reluctantly unfolded the cloak and held it up for Penelope's inspection. "Penelope, is this Niccoli's cloak?" he asked.

Penelope's eyes opened wide and all the color drained from her face as she viewed the cloak. "Yes," she whispered in an almost inaudible voice, "it is Niccoli's. Why did she discard it? What has happened?"

Andros shrugged his shoulders and slowly shook his head. "I have no way of knowing," he replied.

Not only was Andros concerned about Niccoli's welfare, but he also was keenly aware of the punishment that surely would happen to both he and Penelope if they could not find her. He remembered the last words that Senator Cademus had said to them when they departed from Rome. 'You will have to answer to me if anything happens to my daughter,' he had warned. 'A thought that you do not even want to consider!' The words were now ringing loudly in his ears knowing that Niccoli's disappearance may very well be a reality.

He shook his head to clear the memory and focus his full attention back to Penelope. He tried to think of some way to comfort her but what words could ease the despair that they both felt? The only remedy and salvation for them would be if Niccoli herself walked through the door and greeted them. Unfortunately, that was not happening.

By this time Penelope was hysterical. "What are we going to do?" she wailed. "Our deaths have been sealed!" The words seemed to stick in her throat and she could hardly manage to get the last word out before breaking into uncontrollable sobs.

Andros bent down and gently pulled her to her feet.

"Now, now," he spoke softly as he put his arms around her in an effort to comfort her, "don't jump ahead of yourself. Perhaps she has simply spent the night with a friend." Instantly he realized that his words had quite the opposite effect of what he had intended. Not only did they not soothe Penelope but they managed to upset her even more.

"What do you mean?" she screeched as she shoved him away. "Spend the night with a friend! What friend? Who would she stay with that would make her keep her whereabouts a secret from us?"

Her despair was turning into the kind of anger that only frustration can foster. Her eyes narrowed into tiny slits and then, without warning, she let out a piercing scream that caused Andros to quickly put his hands over his ears in order to block out the shrill sound.

"How could she do this to us?" she shrieked. "How dare she be so careless! She knows what her father will do to us if any harm comes to her." She crossed the room, pounded her fists on the table and screamed at the top of her voice, "Niccoli, you are nothing but an inconsiderate wench! You are so spoiled that you think of no one but yourself. Get home this instant! Do you hear me? This instant!"

Even though he could identify with her fright, Andros had never seen Penelope so distraught and it took him by total surprise. "Penelope, for the sake of all the gods in the heavens, calm yourself," he pleaded. But Penelope's hysteria only worsened and he knew that he had to do something more drastic to shock her into quieting down. Putting both hands on her shoulders he shook her hard enough to make her head bobble back and forth. "I said stop it!" his voice was stern and demanding. "You are talking crazy."

Penelope glared at him, her eyes flashing the anger that she felt. "Let go of me!" she demanded in a low threatening voice. When Andros did not release her she started pounding on his chest. "You don't understand," she cried. "Niccoli is gone. We are now the walking dead!"

"Yes, I do understand," replied Andros, "but you are not going to bring her back by being hysterical."

Penelope stared at Andros and gradually her hysteria gave way to gulping sobs. "I know," she lamented, "you are right." She grew limp in Andros' arms and he held her and waited patiently for her to compose herself.

"There is nothing more that we can do tonight," he assured her when she had gained her composure. "I will rise early in the morning and continue my search, but for now we both need to get some rest so that we will be fresh for the tasks that lay ahead of us tomorrow. Everything will work out, you'll see."

Andros was not only trying to convince Penelope not to worry, but also himself. He silently prayed from the depth of his heart that Niccoli would soon be home safe and unscathed. He was well aware that Cornelius loved his daughter more than his very life or status in the Roman community. The fact that Diana, Niccoli's mother, could have no other children made the senator dangerously protective of his daughter. Andros shuddered as he thought of the paternal instincts that Niccoli's disappearance would bring out in Cornelius. He knew that for Penelope's safety, as well as his own, there was no alternative but to find Niccoli alive and well.

* * *

The brilliant sun of early summer streamed down from the heavens and warmed Cornelius, as he stood in the courtyard adjacent to his bedroom. He was confident the Roman Gods had directed the golden rays explicitly for him and he wanted to do everything possible to capture their invigorating energy. He straightened himself to his full height, tilted his face towards the heavens, and clasped his hands behind his back to better open his chest cavity and allow the healing rays to penetrate his entire being.

He believed that at this very moment life was giving him everything he desired. The scent of flowers blooming profusely along the edge of the marble slab filled his nostrils with a sweet fragrance that was unmatched by any other. To better absorb the greatness that surrounded him, he took a deep breath that started from the tip of his toes and filled his body to capacity with the magnificent essence.

He loved the privacy the courtyard provided. It was his favorite hide-away where he could collect his thoughts, energize his entire being and momentarily escape his hectic and demanding life. From its vantage point he could look out over the spectacular city of Rome, capital of the Roman Empire. Oh, how he loved the marble columns, golden statues and elaborate altars built to honor her many pagan gods. Pride filled his breast in knowing he was instrumental in making her the greatest city the world had ever known. A city of power, glory and splendor! A place where the people of status and grandeur had ardent desires to belong.

As far back as he could remember he had known that he wanted to be involved in her growth and have a voice in her government. His dream had become a reality. Not only had he accomplished the feat of being the youngest man to have been appointed to the Roman senate, but he also had gained the respect of his fellow senators. He was a great orator and his voice weighed heavily in all major decisions concerning his beloved city.

His thoughts went back to when he had carefully selected the site upon which to build his home. He had wanted it to reflect his status in the community and had spent more hours than he could count working side by side with the most prominent architect in all of Rome to design the elaborate structure. He meticulously went over every detail and when the spectacular home was completed it included stately columns, marble floors and lush gardens that framed surrounding courtyards.

To make the comfort of his home complete he had acquired the finest servants he could find. He insisted upon loyalty and the ability to do their assigned tasks in a co-operative and efficient manner. Then why, with all of this at her fingertips, had Niccoli been so determined to leave? She had been accustomed to all the luxuries that could be provided her and he could not understand how she could toss everything aside as meaningless. Nor could he understand her strong desire to dance and why she had so stubbornly made up her mind to continue her studies under a woman named Mary who resided in Jerusalem. 'She will round out my abilities as a dancer,' she had told him.

Cornelius had done his best to convince his daughter not to leave. He had searched Rome over in an effort to find another instructor that would be acceptable. But not one of them satisfied her and, as usual, she had broken down his resistance until he had given in to her wishes. He wondered as he stood there if other fathers gave in to their daughters, as he always seemed to do.

Jerusalem! Of all places! How he abhorred the fact that Niccoli had gone there. He cringed at the thought of her associating with such peasants, and felt extremely helpless now that she was so far from his protective reach. Many times he had pondered over how he could protect her from the evils and poverty of others that would surely confront her, but he found few answers.

He did, however, find some consolation in the fact he had sent two of his finest servants, Andros and Penelope, to accompany her. They had been in his service for many years and watched Niccoli grow from an infant. He could think of no others he would entrust with such responsibility. Before they had departed, he instructed them to watch over Niccoli and see to her every need until she would tire of her new adventure and return home.

He longed to see his daughter. Even though she was willful at times, her beauty and grace enhanced his very being. He missed her cheerful greeting when he came home in the evenings and longed to see her gracious smile. She was so full of life and dreams for the future that it reminded him of himself when he was her age.

He thought back to the day of her departure as she waltzed about gathering last minute items for her journey. The sunlight that flooded the room had danced upon her thick raven hair, making it glisten in all of its magnificence as it cascaded in soft waves down her back. Her velvety brown eyes reflected the excitement she felt in knowing that she was about to start a new chapter in her life. He remembered thinking that the Roman gods had most assuredly smiled upon his daughter the day she was born.

As he stood reminiscing, an equally beautiful woman entered his bedroom. The lavender dress she was wearing fell in fluid folds from the golden cord that was tied beneath her breasts. With each step she took she stirred a gentle breeze that caused the soft fabric to mold against her flawless body. Pearls were interwoven in her raven hair and highlighted the streaks of silver that were beginning to appear. Regardless of her age, she was still as beautiful as any goddess could ever hope for.

Diana approached the archway leading to the courtyard and lovingly watched her husband who was totally unaware of her presence. She lingered for a moment and then, with a slight movement of her hand, dismissed his manservant. He respectfully bowed his head and placed the toga, which he held ready for his master, upon the bed. Without a word he quietly backed out of the room and Diana at last was alone with her husband.

"Cornelius, it is time for you to prepare to leave for the senate," she said softly. The sound of her voice brought her husband back to the present. She smiled as he turned to look at her. "You were thinking of Niccoli, weren't you?" she asked. There was a quiet understanding in her voice as she continued, "I, too, miss her. She is always on my mind. I do hope she is happy and safe."

"As do I," replied Cornelius, and then with newfound vigor he rushed on. "Time has gotten away from me; thank you for nudging me." He bent down and kissed his wife on her forehead as he hurriedly brushed past her to don his toga. "I've always prided myself on my punctuality," he boasted, "and today will be no different." A twinkle came to his eyes, and his voice was full of mischief as he continued in a teasing manner, "Of course, we both know that the credit goes to you. What would I do without you?"

"Very well, I'm sure," replied Diana, ignoring his humor.

Cornelius chuckled at his wife. He loved to tease her, but he always made sure she understood his meaning. Her beauty and grace reminded him of a delicate earthen urn that would break into irreparable pieces if not handled with loving care. He was well aware of how demanding a senator's life could be and tried to allow for quality time with her each day. Diana, however, was always gracious about the limited time she had with him and he loved her all the more for it. His heart always had belonged to her and, even though his handsome stature attracted many women easily and his status in the Roman community was alluring to status conscious women, he would never waver from her side. Together, with Niccoli, they were the model Roman family, the envy of many.

The peace that Cornelius and Diana felt would be shattered, like a mirror hurled against a marble wall, had they been aware of Niccoli's disappearance and that Andros was now searching all of Jerusalem for her...their most valuable possession.

CHAPTER 2

Niccoli's journey to Jerusalem had been full of wonder and excitement. From the first moment she embarked upon the ship, the crew and their precision of work awed her as they navigated the ship across the Great Sea; first docking at Sicily, then Crete and Cyprus before they arrived at Judea, their final destination.

Each port had its own mysterious ways. She had not expected to see such vast differences in cultures, and was intrigued by the people's dress and various skin tones. She quickly moved from one thing to another in her eagerness to capture everything there was to see. She did not want to miss one little detail.

Watching over Niccoli kept Andros quite busy. He was totally exhausted by the end of the day and convinced that the young were meant for the young and he longed for his old routine duties, boring as they might seem in comparison.

Niccoli loved the sea. The melodious sound of the waves pounding against the ship's hull was soothing to her and each night as she lay quietly in her bunk; the sound lulled her into a peaceful sleep. The highlight of her travel, however, was to stand on the ship's deck at sunset and feel the sea misting her face. As she stood silhouetted against the hues of the sunset she was totally unaware of how beautiful she was when the wind blew her hair and framed her face in soft gentle waves of motion. It was as though nature had found a new playground on which to orchestrate.

Niccoli had always been fond of the sunset, but on the sea its beauty magnified one hundred fold. To watch the bright orange sun reflect upon the water was beautiful beyond explanation. She marveled at how the ball and its reflection would blend together and then, as if by magic, disappear as one beyond the horizon, leaving behind a velvet blue studded canopy overhead and the sound of waves breaking as the ship cut through the water.

It was such a peaceful time. In Niccoli's mind she imagined music and could see herself dancing before Mary; moving as gracefully as reeds swaying in the gentle breeze and using her hands to tell a story of love. As she stood there on deck she could almost sense the veils floating about her body as she and the music blended together as one.

She could not change, nor did she want to, the overwhelming desire to dance. She knew that most girls her age were already married and had children of their own. It was not as though she hadn't had the opportunities to marry, because there were many young suitors that would have been proud to have her for a wife, but she had no interest in either men or marriage. She saw marriage as an obstacle that would interfere with her aspirations of becoming an accomplished dancer. Her only thoughts centered upon finding new ways to improve the dance steps she already knew, or to conquer new advanced routines. She already was recognized as a fine dancer with great potential; however, to become a student in Mary's prestigious school had not been an easy accomplishment. She first had to be recommended by her Roman instructors, and only then was she eventually considered and accepted by Mary.

Once she arrived in Jerusalem it took little time for her to

settle into a busy routine and with each day there came a new challenge. She found Mary to be an excessively strict taskmaster who did not often give praise, but knew she was pleased with her talent and dedication when she asked her to help with the beginner's class.

Today had been especially hectic. Mary had given her several new dance steps and she was so engrossed in practicing that she did not realize how late it had become. When she finally left the school it was at dusk of early evening and she was now sorry she had earlier instructed Andros to leave on an errand.

The evening air had a chill about it and Niccoli wrapped her indigo blue cloak tightly about her slender body. The lateness of the evening cast long shadows in front of her and she felt very nervous about walking down the dimly lit street. Her tired sore muscles screamed at her and the thought of stretching out in the comfort of her bed made her even more anxious to get home.

She had not gone far when unexpectedly she saw in the twilight shadows the outlines of three men. Their loud singing did not alarm her at first, but her instincts told her danger was approaching when she heard intermittent exclamations of profanities pierce the air whenever anyone would accidentally get in their way. She stopped and pressed herself against the wall. Maybe if she stood very still she could melt into the surroundings and they would pass by without discovering her.

Fear consumed her and she felt her body tremble as her heart pounded in her ears. She was too scared to move or even breathe, for fear of discovery. What would they do if they saw her? Why had she stayed so late at school?

The voices grew louder and Niccoli watched as the men stepped out of the shadows and into the faint light that flickered through a window. A silent scream echoed in her ears and fear turned to panic. "Roman soldiers!" she gasped and threw her hands over her mouth to muffle any sounds that might rise up in her throat. She had heard many stories about drunken soldiers and instinctively she knew that she was in trouble. She had to get away, but how? Quickly she looked about her for an escape route and saw an alley only a few steps away, but to get to it meant that she had to go towards the direction of the men. What if they would see her? Dare she take the risk?

She again looked at the soldiers; they were still huddled together and she could hear them discussing what else they could do to make their evening memorable. Perhaps, if she could slip past them and get lost in the darkness of the alley, she would be able to run to the safety of her home. She decided that the risk was worth it and prayed that they would be so engrossed in their deliberation that they would not notice her.

Slowly she inched her way toward the narrow passageway. It seemed to take an eternity to make any progress and with each step she repeated a prayer of protection to her Roman Gods. Everything was going as planned, only a couple of steps more and she could escape into the darkness.

Suddenly a soldier's voice pierced the air! "Look, Jess!" he yelled. "A beautiful woman about your age! Surely the Gods have dropped her from the heavens especially for you."

Niccoli's heart froze with fear. She needed no explanation of what he was referring to and she sped around the corner, running as fast as she could down the alley. Even though her heart was pounding loudly in her ears she could hear the sound of the three men's heavy footsteps as they ran in close pursuit behind her.

"Oh, please protect me!" she cried to her Gods. But the pounding steps were closing in on her. In a matter of seconds one of the soldiers had gotten past her making the escape route an impossibility. Then, just as quickly as the footsteps had started, they stopped and when she turned about she saw the two other soldiers behind her. Terror stabbed her heart as she realized there was no escaping...she was trapped!

Laughing at his newly found sport, Marcos, the most daring of the three, grabbed Niccoli and spun her around. He held her at arm's length so that he could survey her from head to toe. Judging from the smug look on his face, Niccoli knew that he was extremely pleased with what he had captured. "My, you are a lovely thing!" he exclaimed. The sound of his voice was boastful, as though she was his catch of the day. "Tonight must be our lucky night," he called out to the other two as they drew near.

Focusing his full attention on Niccoli, he whispered in her ear, "You see, my friend Jess has never known a woman. I think you would be the perfect one for him to prove himself a man."

Niccoli could see his broad grin shine through his thick beard as he looked down at her. How dare he touch her or assume he had the right to detain her. When she felt his hand leave her waist and move towards her breasts she quickly thrust it aside.

"Take your hands off me!" she demanded. Her voice seethed with anger and disgust. "Only I will choose the man I want to be with. Not you! The sight of each of you disgusts me!"

In an effort to free herself she pushed against her captor's chest with both hands, but Marcos' strength was too great for her and her struggles meant no more to him than those of a pesky fly. Totally ignoring her, he urged his friends to come closer so they might see more clearly his newly found treasure. "What fire she has," he stated, "and she is as beautiful as any fine horse in Rome."

Marveling at her spunk, he proceeded to walk her around in a large circle in much the same way as one might lead a prize horse. Niccoli twisted and kicked in a vain attempt to rid herself of him, but Marcos only laughed uproariously as he jumped back and successfully held her at arm's length so that her kicks could not connect.

"You swine!" Niccoli shrieked, "you filthy swine." Frantic, she bit his hand long and hard until Marcos finally responded.

"Ow-w-w, you wench!" he yelled out in pain and anger. Instinctively he smacked Niccoli so hard across the face that it made her head snap back from the force of the blow, causing her to fall limp in his arms. He put his bruised and bleeding hand to his mouth and sucked on it to relieve the pain. Even though he was hurting, he still was enticed by the spirit that Niccoli had displayed. Yes, she was indeed a lovely thing, and he was quite confident they would all have to agree on that.

When Niccoli regained her senses, she realized that she was unable to match his strength. She remained quiet and her mind raced as she tried to think of a way to convince them to tire of their game and let her continue on her way. "There must be many other women who could please Jess better than I," she started to reason with them. "Someone with far more experience. One who would be very willing to do whatever you ask."

Niccoli sought some sign from the three to show that they were going to change their minds, but there were no indications of sympathy or willingness to respect her wishes. She could see the younger man's eyes flashing with excitement in anticipation of what he intended to do and she assumed that he was Jess. She needed no convincing to know that he was more than willing to go along with his friends' suggestions.

The third Roman chuckled as he came out of the shadows. "Oh, I'm sure there are many other women. Some even quite beautiful," he smirked, "but you must understand...Jess deserves the one that is best suited for him and we are all in agreement that you are the perfect one for him."

Niccoli glared at him. Even though his voice was gentler

than that of Marcos, she knew he was no different.

"Please, don't tell me you are not willing to please our friend," he continued as he approached her. He nodded for Marcos to release her so that he could take her into his arms. "Now, now, my little wildcat," he whispered softly in her ear. "Calm yourself, for we mean no harm to come to you. We just want to have a good time together. I'm sorry that my friend has not treated you very kindly, but I do hope you will excuse his bad manners. My name is Sal, and what might yours be?"

"Niccoli Cademus," she snapped. His soft-spoken words infuriated her. "My father is Cornelius Cademus, Roman Senator! He will have your head for this, so I would suggest that you let me go."

"Cademus?" Sal repeated and silently questioned, 'Could this possibly be the Roman senator's daughter? Not likely. Why would she be here alone in Jerusalem? If she was his daughter, where was her servant escort?'

While Sal was digesting the name, he unconsciously loosened his grip around Niccoli's waist, and she saw her chance to free herself. With new found strength she broke free, but, in her haste, her cloak fell from her shoulders and onto the dirt of the narrow passageway. "Help me!" she screamed as she ignored her fallen cloak and sped toward the end of the alley. "Oh please, somebody help me!" she pleaded…but there was no one in sight to respond to her cries.

Her freedom was short-lived as Sal caught up with her easily and stepped in front of her to block her escape and again took her into his arms. He gripped her right arm and forced it behind her back, pulling her close to his body. Alarms went off in Niccoli's head as she felt his hard body press against hers. She had to get away! With her free hand she clawed at his eyes and could feel her nails sink into his flesh as they ripped across his face.

"Harlot!" Sal yelled. The sound of anger was heavy in his

voice and all traces of the soft-spoken pretense disappeared. "I'll teach you to never again scratch me!" he bellowed and hit her with such force that it flung her against the wall. Dazed, she slid to the ground in a heap and blood trickled from the corner of her mouth.

"Hey, not so rough," Marcos called out. "Pray, how can she please Jess if you strike her senseless?" He hurried over and bent down to see if she was seriously hurt. "Are you alright?" he questioned.

"Get away from me!" gasped Niccoli.

"She is fine. The fire is still there," laughed Marcos. He put his arm around her waist and picked her up, as if she was a shock of wheat, and carried her over to where Jess was standing in anticipation. He grinned at the young man's excitement and dumped Niccoli at his feet. "Here, she is all yours. Watch out, for she is a little demon!" he laughed uproariously. "You must be careful that she does not kick you where your manhood will hurt the most."

The scene that had just unfolded before Jess's eyes had filled him with a type of excitement he had never before felt. He looked down at Niccoli in a dazed heap at his feet and started ripping the clothes away from her body. He needed no encouragement from his friends to continue the search for this new adventure.

Slowly Niccoli's senses returned and through the haze she could hear the other two men cheer on their friend. Jess' horrible sweaty body lay on top of hers and she could hear his heavy breathing in her ears. And then the pain, the horrible wrenching pain! Her stomach started to heave as waves of nausea flooded over her, and she fought hard to prevent vomiting for fear of choking.

She tried to scream, but the pain overwhelmed her and no sound came forth. She strained to pull herself out from under his weight, but he was not at all willing to allow his captive treasure to escape. He grabbed both of her hands and held them high above her head until she was pinned to the ground even more securely. Her chest ached from his weight and she couldn't breathe. She felt she would surely smother, and wondered where were her Roman Gods when she needed them? Why didn't they come to her rescue?

Just as Niccoli felt there was no hope she saw a reflection of light bounce off the knife that Jess had stripped from his waist and tossed aside. She knew she must somehow get to it and quickly put a plan together. If she quit fighting and lay perfectly still perhaps she could put him off guard.

"I'll fight you no more," she whispered in his ear. "You have proven yourself quite a man."

Jess smiled and kissed her upon her lips. He released her hands to allow him the pleasure of caressing her breasts. That was all Niccoli needed! Before Jess could fathom what was happening, she had pulled the knife from its sheath and plunged it deep into his side.

Jess screamed out in pain, and Niccoli quickly rolled his body off of her and staggered to her feet. With the knife still in her hand she looked for the other two rogues, and saw them running to their friend's aid. They had momentarily forgotten her, and now was her chance for freedom!

Even though she was stripped of most of her clothing, she again headed for the end of the alley. However, she had taken only a few steps before she felt herself being hurled to the ground. She looked up to see Marcos standing over her in the kind of anger she had never before seen. His eyes were glazed over and she knew that he was completely out of control; she was totally at his mercy.

Marcos looked down at the knife still clutched in her hand. With a loud yell he stomped on her hand and proceeded to grind it into the dirt in much the same way as one would kill a poisonous bug to make sure it was quite dead. He kicked the knife out of her hand and she screamed out in pain.

Knowing that she was once again defenseless she sobbed in

a barely audible voice, "Please, somebody help me...please."

Marcos picked up the knife and hovered over her. He watched her eyes as they followed the gleam of the blade that he moved back and forth only inches above her face. He was so enraged that he barely heard her pleading for her life. All he could think of was that she would not give in to their desires and his friend was now bleeding and perhaps dying because of her.

Niccoli could see that his jaws were clamped together with such force that his jawbone made a defined impression through his cheeks. His voice was low and threatening as he spoke through the clenched teeth. "Beg all you want," he hissed, "it makes no difference. I'm going to see that you never entice another man! They won't even want to lay their eyes upon you when I'm finished."

With one sweeping stroke of the knife he slashed her across the cheek. Niccoli screamed out and threw her hand up to her cheek. She could feel the blood run between her fingers and the full realization that she was now fighting for her life filled her with terror. With an adrenalin rush she grabbed Marcos' arm and, as if by some miracle, she was able to pull it to her mouth. She sank her teeth deep into his wrist, but instead of forcing him to release her she only succeeded in making him even angrier. With his other arm he gave such a severe blow to her neck that she thought her head would explode. She could neither breathe nor utter a sound. Through the haze she could hear him cursing her for the pain she had caused him and felt the knife repeatedly slash at her face and breasts. Soon the haze turned into blackness and she lay motionless as her blood flowed from her body and formed puddles that stained the dirt around her.

"Stop!" yelled Sal, "Have you lost your senses? For the love of the Gods, contain yourself." Sal was beside himself with the fear of discovery and ran back to help Jess. "Hurry, Marcos!" he yelled over his shoulder, "We must leave before

31

someone comes in response to her screams."

Marcos looked at the motionless woman lying in the dirt before him and suddenly the full realization of the horrific act that he had just committed shocked him back to reality. Horror gripped him, as he looked first at the knife in his hand and then back to the slashed body of a once beautiful woman. Filled with overwhelming guilt he flung the knife aside as though it was a hot poker and exploded with a piercing scream that not only penetrated the alley around him but also the heavens above him.

"Marcos, you are a fool!" Sal accused. He loathed his friend's temper. It was always getting them into trouble. Right now he would like nothing better than to go over and punch him in the face, but there was not enough time to indulge in the fulfillment of such a pleasure. "Forget about her," he yelled, "get your miserable uncontrollable self over here and help me with Jess!"

Marcos looked at his friends and struggled to pull himself together. In a daze he helped Sal get Jess up on his feet and by placing his arms around their necks they were able to half carry and half drag him from the alley; never taking the time to look back at the crumpled and bleeding heap they were leaving behind. Perhaps they would be able to forget what had happened if they could erase from their memory the sight of the disfigured body.

Their carefree drunken evening had turned into a horrible nightmare filled with terror and assault.

CHAPTER 3

The full moon shone brightly over the city of Jerusalem, making the simple clay houses glisten in its radiance. There was now a quiet hush over the city and the splendor of the night gave way to the illusion of peace and tranquility. A women's voice could be heard urging her husband to quicken his pace along the dusty narrow street. Two Roman soldiers, supporting a seemingly drunken comrade, brushed past the Hebrew couple and disappeared into the quiet night, which only moments before had been pierced with the cries of a woman pleading for help.

"Jacob, for goodness sakes, can't you move any faster?" she asked impatiently. His indifference irritated her and it reflected in her voice. The fire of justice still burned brightly in her soul even though her black hair was beginning to show a little gray and, over the years, she had put on 'a meager amount' of weight. She was an obedient woman but there were times when she thought that her husband, handsome as he was, had to be the slowest man that God had ever created. She glared at him as he sauntered towards her. She muttered under her breath and, trying hard to be the obedient wife, waited for him to catch up with her. When he was at her side she wanted to scream out 'finally, you have

33

caught up with me' but instead she fought to remain calm and only said, "That poor woman is in serious trouble and we must quickly find her."

Jacob was indeed reluctant to get involved in something he felt was none of their business because, in his mind, he was sure it was nothing more than a family dispute. But, as he had come to realize over the years, there was no stopping Sarah when she put her mind to something, a fact that often angered him because it seemed to be far beyond his control. Why should things be different this evening when she had not changed in all of their fifteen years of marriage? In his opinion, however, she definitely overextended her boundaries.

"Would you please stay behind me," he pleaded. He could see clearly that if he did not relent to her wishes she would continue on without him. "Sarah, please listen to me. If you insist upon getting involved at least let me go before you and see what the trouble might be."

Jacob looked at his wife and fought back the urge to shake her for being so stubborn. He felt sure in his heart that there would be a time her zeal would get him into more trouble than he cared to think about. It was not that he was afraid, he was a big man and could hold his own in a fight, but he always preferred to avoid confrontation if at all possible. Going into the dark alley that his wife was urging him to enter was not to his liking, and definitely not his way of avoiding danger.

Sarah obediently complied with her husband's request and returned to stand at his side. She could see his impatience with her and tried to understand his hesitance. If she were truthful with herself she would have to admit that in her efforts to help others she might at times have overstepped her bounds, which could have put him in danger. She quickly said a prayer of thanksgiving to God that Jacob was a patient man.

The alley was dark and forbidding and it took a few

minutes for their eyes to adjust to the darkness, however, everything seemed to be peaceful enough. "I don't see anything out of the ordinary," Jacob finally commented to Sarah. He felt relieved when she finally nodded in agreement, but, as he put his arm around her waist to leave, she suddenly stopped and cocked her head to one side. Jacob's heart sank. He knew avoidance had been too good to be true.

"Listen, Jacob," she whispered, trying to discern what she had just heard. "Did you hear that?"

"Yes, I heard," responded her husband. "It was just a kitten. You know how many cats there are around here. Anyway, I don't hear anything now." Jacob was beginning to get a little more than agitated and wanted to return home. "Sarah, please, you can see for yourself there is no one here," he stated firmly. He did not want to risk any further involvement and the sooner they left the area the better he would like it.

"I don't think so," mused Sarah, "I can sense something terribly wrong. Please go into the alley, if only for a short distance, and see what you can find." As she spoke she pushed her husband forward in an effort to get him to continue his search.

"Sarah, why can't you mind you own business?" grumbled Jacob. "Why are you so determined to get me into trouble?" She undoubtedly had to be the most stubborn woman he had ever known.

Grumbling to himself he moved down the narrow passageway. Suddenly something caught his attention. Perhaps the wind had blown some trash along the side of the building, or maybe a beggar had found a comfortable spot for the night. Whatever it was he felt drawn to it.

His body was flexed and ready for the unexpected as he cautiously approached the suspicious heap. Then he heard it again, another faint cry. This time, however, it sounded more like a moan and he cautiously bent down to get a better look.

What he saw startled him so much that his heart skipped a beat and he quickly jumped back in shock. Lying before him was the naked body of a woman! A women who was bleeding profusely from the numerous knife slashes that had been inflicted upon her upper body and face.

"Oh, blessed Jehovah, have mercy upon us," he whispered. He felt himself shaking as he knelt beside her. He could only guess at the terror and brutality that had just occurred. He quickly surveyed the situation and could see the blood staining the ground around the girl and instinctively knew that he must not waste one precious moment of this girl's life. He quickly wrapped his cloak tightly around the still body, scooped her into his arms and started running from the horrible scene with the limp body dangling in his arms; leaving a trail of blood behind as it flowed rapidly from her body. With every step that he took he fervently prayed to God that it was not too late to save the unfortunate victim.

Sarah took one look and ran ahead to their nearby home to start ripping bandages. When Jacob arrived with the victim he rushed past her and laid the once beautiful girl upon the table near the hearth.

"Dear merciful God! Look at the blood all over your clothes, Jacob. What in this world has happened?" questioned Sarah.

"I can only guess," replied Jacob as he removed his cloak from the unconscious body. What the light of the fire revealed made him realize that the situation was much worse than he had imagined. The body lying before him had been slashed beyond recognition. The gaping wounds about the face and breasts were bleeding profusely. The fingers on her hand were smashed so badly the flesh was pulled away from the broken bones. Never before had he seen such desecration of another human.

"How can one person be so brutal to another?" Sarah cried. Her faced flushed with anger at the thought of what must have happened. She would never understand the cruelty that went on about her. Hurriedly she started pouring wine over the gaping wounds. She had tended to the injured before and knew what needed to be done, but in this case she was not sure that she would be able to stop the bleeding in time to save the girl. A feeling of inadequacy flooded over her.

"Jacob, you must help me," she instructed. "Press the sides of the wounds together as best you can so that I can bind them. Be careful!" she cautioned. "Match up the sides before you press them together. She is already going to be horribly scarred, so don't do anything to make it worse."

No matter what they did, or how fast they worked, it seemed as though the bleeding would not subside. Sarah was getting very frustrated. "Press harder, Jacob!" The urgency in Sarah's voice made it sound demanding. "She is losing too much blood. If we don't get it stopped soon she is surely going to die."

Minutes seemed like hours before the blood soaked bandages did their job, and the bleeding finally subsided. At last, it appeared as though they had won their first battle.

"Sarah," Jacob said softly, "you have done everything you know to do. Now it is up to her and God. I do hope she is a fighter." Jacob knew how hard Sarah had worked to save her patient. In spite of how hopeless the situation might be he was quite sure that Sarah would blame herself if they could not save the girl.

"Have I told you today how much I love you?" he asked in a gentle voice and put his arms around her to hold her tight.

"Yes, but you can tell me again; I won't mind," she sighed as she looked up at her husband and smiled. She laid her head on his shoulder and patted his hand as they held each other close. The joy and contentment they felt because of their love and devotion for each other was in sharp contrast to the terror of what had happened in an abandoned alley to the unidentified girl who was so desperately fighting for her life.

Jacob thought of the probable dark future that lay ahead for their patient and how much healing she would need. Not only for her outward wounds, but for the deep wounds that would surely scar her heart.

Soon the dark of the black night gave way to the dawn of a new day, one that would begin a time in which Niccoli would have to face the experience of emotions she had never felt before; those of extreme anger, guilt, ugliness, hopelessness and depression to name a few.

Days turned into weeks as Jacob watched his wife nurse her patient back to health. He could see the love and concern that she was feeling for the young woman, and knew that if it had not been for her this stranger would have bled to death in the darkness of an abandoned alley.

CHAPTER 4

A week had gone by and, even though his search was ceaseless, Andros still was unable to find Niccoli. He had exhausted every possible lead and he knew that it was time for both he and Penelope to face the inevitable task of making a decision on how to handle the situation. He came to the conclusion that there were two possible solutions: one, they go to Cornelius and tell him about the disappearance of his only child and risk probable death, or two, they could run away and hopefully find a safe place to hide before Cornelius became aware of her disappearance. After careful deliberation, complicated by Penelope's hysteria, it was decided that out of love for Niccoli, they would send word to Cornelius in the hope he would be able to accomplish that which they had been unable to do. However, for their own safety, they would pack the few belongings they owned and slip way before he could administer their punishment.

Meanwhile, in Rome, Cornelius was oblivious to what was happening in Jerusalem and was enjoying a sauna in the steam house with a few select Senators. He poured another dipper of water over the hot rocks in the center of the room, leaned forward and inhaled the hissing steam. He savored the total relaxation and feeling that every pour of his flesh was clean and refreshed. He was only half listening to the others discuss Senator Thadious' latest romance and, trying to ignore them as much as possible, stretched out on the bench and closed his eyes in an effort to block out their conversation. There were times his peers bored him with their petty gossip and today ranked high upon his list for boring.

Suddenly, they were interrupted with loud voices outside the door. The Senators sat upright, irritated that anyone would dare to disturb them but also alert to the fact that any one of them could have an enemy who would like to detach their heads and roll them down the streets of Rome. All eyes were on the door as it opened and they breathed a sigh of relief when they saw the guard was unscathed and standing at attention before them.

"Forgive me," he said, "I did not wish to interrupt, but there is a messenger who insists he has an urgent message for Senator Cademus."

Cornelius halfheartedly motioned for the messenger to enter. He too, was irritated with the interruption and could not imagine anything so important that could not wait for another half hour.

"He is from Jerusalem," the guard informed him.

"Jerusalem?" Cornelius repeated questioningly. His full attention was now on the messenger as he rose to his feet, 'What urgent message from Jerusalem would be directed to me,' he thought to himself, 'except perhaps word from my daughter. What is wrong with my daughter!'

The thought of something happening to Niccoli startled him and he precariously leaped across the hot coals to seize the scroll from the messenger's hand. His fingers trembled as he unrolled the parchment and the color drained from his face as he read and then reread the scribbled words.

Suddenly his thoughts were jumping to all kinds of conclusions and he cried out in anguish, "No, this can not be true!" The realization that he may never again see his daughter made Cornelius' stomach twist into a tight knot. From deep within he groaned the questions, 'Where is Niccoli now? Where was Andros when she needed him?'

The other Senators silently sat huddled together around the hot stones and watched Cornelius pace back and forth; extremely curious as to what was happening. They had never seen Cornelius in such a rage and, even thought they wanted to ask about the content of the message, their instincts told them to not question him while he was so obviously upset. Suddenly, without warning, they were forced to quickly duck flying embers as Cornelius furiously flung the scroll into the pit of hot coals and bolted out the door.

They breathlessly waited until Cornelius had turned the corner and then, like little children, commanded Anthony to hurriedly retrieve the scroll from the hot coals before it burst into flames. With great caution he hurriedly complied and flicked the scroll out of the pit onto the floor; first blowing upon it and then fanning it until the parchment was cool enough to handle. All eyes were upon him as he stretched it open, cleared his throat and began reading aloud: "Your daughter has disappeared. My efforts to find her have proven fruitless....Andros." Anthony looked at the other Senators, "It is no wonder that Cornelius was so angry," he affirmed, "given the same situation, I would kill Andros immediately." The others nodded their heads in agreement and confided that they certainly did not envy the position that had fallen upon Andros.

Cornelius could think of nothing, not even Roman politics that could compare to Niccoli's well being and all he was concerned about was getting to Jerusalem as quickly as possible. It was not until he was headed home did his thoughts switch to Diana. He knew how she would react to the news and realized that he had to approach the situation with great care. He paced the outer courtyard while trying to select the right words but finally decided there were no words that could ease the devastation she would feel and that by delaying what had to be done would only cause him more anguish.

He opened the door, took off his cloak and held it out for the servant who greeted him. "Where is my wife?" he asked rather abruptly.

"She is in the garden with a few of her friends, Master," was the response, "do you wish me to tell her of your arrival?"

"No, I will go to her," replied Cornelius. Taking in a long deep breath he reluctantly headed for the garden; knowing in his heart that he would rather take forty lashes across his back than to tell Diana that her daughter had disappeared.

Diana looked up from her conversation with the ladies and smiled when she saw her husband. "Cornelius, you're home early. What a pleasant surprise," she said cheerfully and excused herself from the others to rush over and kiss her husband on the cheek, but she stopped short when she saw the look on his face. "Cornelius, what is it?" she whispered.

"Shhh, tell your friends to go," responded Cornelius. "I have something to tell you."

Shaken, but not wanting her guests to be aware of it, she turned to them and announced pleasantly, "Ladies, as you can see, my husband has returned home and I would like to take advantage of his early arrival, as it does not happen often. Please do not be offended when I ask you to come back another time. To make up for my rudeness, I promise to have my servants prepare something very special for the next time that you are here." She smiled; pretended nothing was wrong and chatted with each of them as she escorted them to the door. After saying the final farewell she turned and hurried back to Cornelius.

"Cornelius, what has happened?" she asked and her voice reflected the uneasiness that she felt in the pit of her stomach.

"Come, let us set on the bench under the olive tree," he suggested as he took her by the arm. "Diana, you are a wonder with your garden, it is especially beautiful this year and you should be very proud," he boasted.

Diana nodded, not at all interested in his small talk, and did not take her eyes off of his face as he gently sat her down and knelt on the ground beside her. He looked down at her tiny hands that lay trembling in her lap and took them into his own.

"It is about Niccoli," he said quietly and watched her stiffen as she waited for him to finish his sentence. He prepared himself for the worst and continued, "I got a message from Andros about an hour ago, he informed us that she never returned home...Diana, she has disappeared!"

Diana's huge brown eyes fixed upon Cornelius and then very quietly, without a word, she closed them and slumped over in a faint. Cornelius took her in his arms and held her against his breast until she slowly regained consciousness and started to cry softly. He rocked her in his arms until she was able to speak, "How are we ever going to get her back?" she asked in an almost inaudible voice.

"I will go to Jerusalem immediately," replied Cornelius. "I have already made the arrangements."

"I want to go with you," Diana said, sitting up now without her husband's help.

"I think it better that you stay home," replied Cornelius, "I can travel faster alone."

"That may be, but I beseech you, my husband, please allow me to go with you," Diana pleaded. "I cannot stay behind not knowing what is happening."

"Oh, Diana...do not do this to me."

"Cornelius, I can not stay behind!" she insisted.

"Very well," he relented, convinced of how intolerable the unknown would be for her.

"We should never have allowed her to go, you know it is our fault that she is missing," Diana lamented.

"Be that as it may, we can not undo that which has already been done," replied Cornelius.

Early the next morning Diana and Cornelius boarded the ship to start their long journey to Jerusalem. They were totally oblivious to how God was watching over Niccoli, even though she was not a believer, and how His Grace had lead Sarah and Jacob to care for her. Because of that loving care, she was now recovered enough to instruct Jacob to send a message informing her parents of where she was staying. It would be a message that would never reach them but simply pass in the night as each went to their assigned destinations.

When their ship docked at the port city of Caesarea, Diana surveyed the surroundings and shuddered. Cornelius had told her that the city would be far different from Rome, but she had not prepared herself for the poverty that existed in this far away place. There were no paved streets, to which she was accustomed, nor any beautiful horses pulling gilded chariots through the streets.

"Oh Cornelius, the homes are made from dirt!" exclaimed Diana. "Is this what Niccoli is living in?"

"Yes, I am afraid it is," replied Cornelius, "Did I not tell you that this area was a flea bitten, desert ravaged and reject laden land? Now you fully understand why I was so adamant about Niccoli not coming here, but, as you know, there was no convincing her that Rome was a far better place. She is the most strong-willed female I have ever known!"

"Yes, somewhat. I think that she takes after her father."

"Diana, how can you say such a thing?" he quipped and then added, "I say she may have a little of her mother's stubbornness.

"Cornelius, I am not stubborn!"

"Be that as it may," laughed Cornelius, "we cannot change things now and we need to continue on our way. Since there was no time to ask Pilot to send an escort, I will have to bargain for some slaves to help us. Perhaps the merchant over there will be able to direct us to someone who is willing to sell horses that we can use for the remaining journey to

Jerusalem. You stay here and I will return in a short while.

"You are going to leave me alone?" gasped Diana.

"I will be where you can see me and well within hearing range."

Diana nodded, and sat down upon the baggage where she could watch her husband. She saw the merchant bow to Cornelius as he approached, and nodded his head as he listened to what Cornelius was requesting. He motioned for another man to join them, and soon the three were engrossed in a series of gestures and bargaining jargon. Finally Cornelius shook hands with the two and returned to Diana.

"There is no cart to be found," he informed her. "We will have to ride donkeys. I realize that you have never ridden a donkey before; do you think you will be able to tolerate it until we get to Jerusalem? I am so sorry to make you have to do this Diana, but I tried to warn you."

"It will be alright, Cornelius," she said in an effort to console her husband. "I am strong and very willing. Niccoli is all that matters, so let us hurry and be on our way."

Cornelius had always marveled how Diana was able to adapt to any situation that she had to accept. He knew of no other woman, except for his stubborn Niccoli, which would do such a thing. Most wives that he had met were spoiled and frigid, a far cry from his warm and loving Diana.

"I have also hired a guide to help us," he continued. "He seems rough and ready for the journey ahead. His name is James, a fisherman on his way to Jerusalem. He is checking for a place for us to stay the night. In the meantime, are you hungry? We can nibble on something while we wait."

"That would be nice, I am starved," agreed Diana.

Cornelius looked around for some shade and saw an olive tree close by.

"Look, there is some shade, it is close enough that we can rest, eat, and still be able to watch over our baggage."

"I would certainly welcome some shade," said Diana, "I

can not believe how hot the sun gets here."

"Yes, this is a pitiful God deserted place. I despise the very sight and smell of it," replied Cornelius as he unpacked some dried meat.

"Relax, my husband," Diana said lovingly, "save your energy for the search."

It was not long before James returned with news. "I have checked with the innkeeper and there is room for the two of you tonight," he informed them. "I will arrange for your baggage to be taken there, so get a good night's sleep for we will need an early start in the morning; preferably at dawn. I take my leave now, see you tomorrow."

"Do you think we can trust him?" asked Diana after he had gone.

"We have little choice, but he seems nice enough and he always looked me straight in the eye when he spoke. I think he will do just fine."

The morning could not come fast enough for Diana. In her anxiety to find Niccoli she had been awake most of the night. "Cornelius," she said with a gentle nudge, "it is time to get up. James will be here very soon."

"I just got to sleep," groaned Cornelius. "How did you sleep?"

"Not well," replied Diana.

There was a knock at the door and Cornelius dragged himself out of bed to answer it. "Good morning, James," Cornelius said as he rubbed sleep from his yes.

"Shalom," replied James. "I will meet you outside in the courtyard when you are ready."

"We will be there." affirmed Cornelius and then turned to Diana. "It will not be long now until we will see Niccoli."

"Oh, I do hope that will be true."

James had the baggage loaded on the pack donkey and was impatiently waiting for Diana and Cornelius. He did not have to wait long, however, before they joined him and when Diana saw the donkeys she started laughing. "You want me to ride on that small animal? Cornelius, you are much to large to ride upon its back."

"They are much stronger than they look," James interjected. "Are you ready?"

"We are ready," replied Cornelius. "Diana, let me help you to get on the donkey."

"Yes, I am afraid I need a lot of help! How do I sit upon one of these animals?"

"With both of your legs on one side," explained Cornelius, "as I am sure you have seen the peasant women in Rome ride."

"Yes, but not I," said Diana nervously. Somehow she managed to get on and stay atop the animal, but, when she tried to get it to move, it just stood still. "What do I do now?" she asked.

"Nothing, I will lead him for a way until you get use to him," laughed James as he took the reins. "Sometimes these donkeys are very stubborn."

Somehow James had managed to get everybody organized and headed down the road. He just shook his head and wondered why these novice people had ever left Rome.

"Tell me James," Cornelius inquired, "do you fish in the Mediterranean Sea for a living?"

"No, I normally fish in the Sea of Galilee. I came here only to visit a friend and to pick up some fishing nets," he said and pointed to the bundle on his donkey. "Why, if I may ask, are you going to Jerusalem? It is a long distance from Rome. Are you a Roman government representative?"

"No, even though it is true that I am a Roman Senator, we have personal reasons for being here," replied Cornelius. "We have a daughter that insisted upon coming here to study dancing under a woman called Mary. She lives in Jerusalem. You do not by chance know of her?"

"Mary...I do not remember such a woman, but there are

many named Mary."

"That is too bad, I was hoping that you would. You see, my daughter has disappeared and we have come to search for her. We have no knowledge of where she might be or what has happened to cause her disappearance."

"I am sorry to hear of this. I know many people; perhaps I can be of some help to you. I will inquire of them when we arrive in Jerusalem."

"That would be very gracious of you," said Diana, appreciative of any help that he might give her.

"It would be my pleasure."

They traveled the rest of the day with little conversation and Diana tolerated the donkey ride without complaint. She was, however, very stiff and sore when they stopped to bed down for the night, another new experience for her.

"Cornelius, I can not lay upon the ground!" she protested. "There are too many bugs, spiders, and worst of all, snakes crawling about!"

"Diana, there is no other choice. I will stretch my cloak down for you to rest upon. I know that you are tired so just quietly bed down," the day's strain shown in Cornelius' voice.

"You don't need to be gruff with me!" pouted Diana.

"Just lie down," Cornelius responded as he waved her off.

"I will! Take your old cloak for yourself!" she shouted as she flung it towards Cornelius and plopped herself upon the bare ground, "I need it not!"

The night was unbearable for Diana. With each noise that she heard she sat upright, waiting to ward off anything that was about to jump out of the darkness and pounce upon her. She finally fell asleep in the wee hours of the morning only to be awakened by the cracking of a branch. She lay very quiet, conscious of every movement around her as she held her breath and kept her eyes wide open. Suddenly, out of the shadows she saw movement. "Cornelius!" she screamed as she sprang to her feet only seconds before two men jumped out of the darkness.

Thanks to Diana's warning, Cornelius and James were alerted to the enemy and able to spring to their feet with their knives drawn before the attackers were upon them.

"Leave us!" James warned the attackers. "We do not wish any harm to come to you."

"Maybe you do not want to harm them, but I want a piece of them," yelled Cornelius, as he crouched down and held his knife out ready to take a slice out of anyone who came near.

The four glared at each other and then, without warning, one of the robbers lunged forward at Cornelius. But Cornelius was ready for battle, and when he took a swipe with his knife he felt it slash the flesh of the robber's arm.

"You son of a jackal! I'll get you for that!" screamed the robber as he again lunged forward, knocking Cornelius to the ground and landing on top of him. The two wrestled as the robber fought to thrust his knife into Cornelius' chest.

Diana was standing close by, "Cornelius, be careful!" she screamed as she watched them struggle.

The two men, each staring into the other's eyes, never let their gaze falter but Cornelius knew that he had the best of the aggressor when his arm started to quiver. In a matter of seconds he had the robber's arm pinned behind his back and was pulling him to his feet.

"James, tell your man that I will slit this one's throat if he continues fighting."

"I think that the fight has gone out of him," replied James.

"I say pin them to the nearest tree. What say you?" asked Cornelius.

"I say brand them a thief," responded James. "Diana, would you gather some wood for a fire?"

Diana nodded and wondered what he had meant, 'brand them a thief'?

Soon the fire was raging and Diana watched as James put the pointed end of a stick into the fire until the end was a glowing red ember. He pulled it out and blew on it; making it glow even brighter to show the robbers just how hot the stick could get. He approached the younger of the two and pointed the glowing stick at his forehead.

"No! Please have mercy on me!" the young man begged.

"Why?" asked James, "Did you have mercy on us?"

"No, for that I am sorry! I tell you, my heart was not into robbing you. I promise I will never rob again!" he cried and fell sobbing at James' feet.

"Then go, find other friends. Never associate with this man again," James ordered. He turned towards the other robber. "You, what do you have to say for yourself?" he demanded. "Did you not taunt this young man into doing your bidding?"

"No, not I, I would never do such a thing. Robbing you was all his idea!"

"I believe you not, it is you who is guilty," rebuked James.

"No, it is not true, I am innocent of any wrong doing."

"You lie!" roared James and struck the robber's forehead with the hot poker. The smell of burnt flesh filled the air. "Now, all can see what you really are...a liar and a thief! Go, while your life is spared."

"No! No! What have you done?" he screamed as he ran away.

Cornelius watched as the two disappeared into the early morning light. "You were much too easy on them," he declared.

"They will rob no more," answered James. "That is what is important."

"Well, so much for an exciting night. I am relieved it is over," stated Diana.

"Diana, if it had not been for you we may have not been able to fight off those robbers," said James. "Thank you for being so alert."

"I was having trouble sleeping," replied Diana. "I guess

that was a good thing now that I look back on it. Anyway, it is over and we are without a blemish. I don't know about you, but I am anxious to continue on to Jerusalem."

"Your wish is my thought exactly," replied Cornelius, "let us pack up and be going."

The rest of the journey was uneventful. James was rather quiet and Cornelius, along with Diana, was thinking about Niccoli and how they would retrace her steps to find out where and why she had disappeared.

When they arrived in Jerusalem, Cornelius thanked James for helping them and took his pouch out to pay him.

"No, I do not need your money," said James. "I was glad for the company. I will ask around for anyone that might have seen your daughter. I hope when you find Niccoli, everything will be well with her."

"Thank you for your concern but you must let me pay you. We agreed upon a price and you must accept it," argued Cornelius.

"No, I do not want it," replied James again.

"You have proven yourself a good friend," Cornelius replied gratefully as he held out his hand in friendship, "and I will never forget it."

"Shalom," replied James as he pressed Cornelius' hand and nodded to Diana.

"Farewell," said Diana. The couple stood and watched until James disappeared among the busy throng of people.

"Where do we go from here?" asked Diana.

"To Mary's studio," was the answer.

Diana looked around at the crude clay homes, the dusty streets and the abundance of beggars and shuddered. "Just what kind of home did you select for our Niccoli?" she asked.

"It is close by, we will go there when we leave Mary's," Cornelius answered almost automatically as he led Diana down a narrow street; finally stopping in front of a small door that was crudely made of heavy timbers. A small sign hung to the side of the door that simply stated: Mary's School of Dancing.

"We have arrived," stated Cornelius as he knocked on the door of the studio.

"Yes, why are you bothering me at this hour?" scolded Mary when she opened the door, but her tone changed when she recognized Cornelius. "Oh, Senator Cademus," she said with a smile, "please come in. It is a pleasure to see you."

"Thank you. This is Diana, my wife and Niccoli's mother."

"You must be here to see Niccoli? I have not seen her for quite some time now. What is she doing?"

"We do not know. I just received word that she had disappeared and we immediately came here to find her."

"Disappeared?" questioned Mary; shocked to hear the news. "It is true that I have not seen her for quite some time but I did not know that she had disappeared."

"Then you can not help me?"

"No, I only know that she left the studio late on the last night that I saw her and she has never been back," responded Mary.

"Thank you for your time," replied Diana despairingly.

"I am so sorry," sympathized Mary.

Cornelius nodded his head in acknowledgement of Mary's concern, his heart heavy with grief.

"What are we to do?" asked Diana after Mary had closed the door.

"We will go to her home, maybe she is there by now."

"Oh, I hope so!"

Cornelius took Diana's arm and they proceeded to the house that he had purchased for Niccoli only a few weeks prior. He prayed to his Gods that they would find Niccoli well and healthy, but his heart was telling him that the chances of finding Niccoli were getting slimmer with each passing hour.

"This is her home," he declared as he pointed to the small

structure in front of him. "Look the door is open! What luck, perhaps she is here!"

Diana ran for the door calling out excitedly, "Niccoli, it is Mother! Where are you...." Her voice faltered and she stopped abruptly in the doorway. The house had been ransacked! The only thing left was a chair that looked as though it had been tossed aside and had landed precariously on one leg, bracing itself against the wall in the corner.

Diana looked hopelessly at her husband. "What has happened?" she asked.

"Poachers, I would imagine," mumbled Cornelius. "It is certain that Niccoli has not been here for awhile, nor Penelope or Andros. Wait until I get my hands on those two! They will wish they had never seen me!"

"I do not want to see them ever again!" sobbed Diana. What more could she do to find her daughter? Where else could she look?

Cornelius just stood motionless in the middle of the room, all that he could think of was how he had failed his daughter.

For the next month they looked for Niccoli, seeking her face in every woman that walked past, looking down all alleys, in the outlying areas, and asking every merchant that they saw if they had seen her; but they found no leads and all hope faded. The agony of waiting would remain their constant companion and with heavy hearts they returned to Rome.

CHAPTER 5

The fact that Niccoli was a stranger to Jacob and Sarah never influenced the way in which they nursed and cared for her. They lovingly saw to her every need, just as though she had always been a dear friend. However, the way in which her wounds healed had been far beyond their control. A once beautiful, vivacious and talented young woman was now cursed with grotesque scars about her face and bosom. Her hand was so twisted and disfigured that it hung inoperative at her side. With each day she became more despondent and no matter what Jacob or Sarah said to encourage her, it had little affect upon her.

"A dancer can not be a dancer unless she can tell a story with her hands," Niccoli would repeat time and again in response to their encouragement. She was filled with insurmountable hate and anger whenever she thought of the Roman soldiers and would spend many sleepless night fanaticizing about how she could torture them. She would set by the window, totally withdrawn into her own world of escape and protection, and ask herself the same questions over and over again, 'Why me? I never harmed them. Why did they do this to me? I do not understand how such a thing could happen to me when I did nothing to deserve it. How could they be so cruel to me!' However, her questions always remained unanswered, and not only did she feel betrayed by her fellow man but she also felt betrayed by her Roman Gods. They did not come to her aid when she needed their help so desperately.

"Why did my Gods forsake me?" she cried aloud one afternoon as she paced from one side of the room to the other.

Sarah looked up from her mending and pondered over Niccoli's question. She had been quietly watching her pace and her heart went out to the girl. She wished that she had an answer, but she did not.

"I do not know," she replied, "such things are beyond my comprehension, but there is a man who might be able to answer your question. He is saying that there is only one merciful God and that even the Roman Gods bow down to Him. Some call Him the Son of God and He is believed to be the promised Messiah. His name is Jesus and He has healed the blind, the lepers, and the crippled. Perhaps He could heal you."

"Heal me?" Niccoli cried out loudly. "How can He heal when He could not stop what the Roman soldiers did to me? Was He merciful then? No! He is no better than my Roman gods. I saw no mercy from Him or any other god when all of this was happening to me." Niccoli's voice was harsh with bitterness as she made a gesture toward her face and hand. "Talk not to me about mercy!" she screamed as she burst into uncontrollable sobs and flung herself upon her bed.

Sarah felt so helpless as she compassionately watched Niccoli vent her frustrations. Because she did not know what to do for her, she allowed her the freedom to express herself in any way needed. She hoped that it would help Niccoli to free herself of the anger and hurt that was so deeply imbedded within. It grieved her to see so much pain in the young woman; no one deserved what she had endured. She waited until Niccoli had fallen asleep before placing a blanket over her, and as she bent down to kiss her upon the cheek she prayed that somehow sleep would help heal the despairing girl's inner wounds. "If anyone deserves a little help it is Niccoli," she thought to herself. "Perhaps Jesus will be the one to make it happen."

* * *

The pain of losing both her beauty and dance abilities were almost more than Niccoli could bear. Never before had she experienced such depression, and today was no different from any other. The weight of her depression fell heavily about her as she half-heartedly climbed the stairs to the upper room of her friends' home. It was there, only a few days prior that Jacob had built a lean-to for her and the shady spot had become her favorite place for refuge.

She crossed over and sat down upon the mat that had been placed beneath the sloping roof. She was totally oblivious to the birds that were singing around her and to the gentle breeze that so graciously fanned her. The sound of children playing in the street below filled the air with gladness, but all she could focus upon was the ugly hand that lay motionless in her lap. How she hated the sight of it. The twisted fingers reminded her of a monster's claw from the mystical past.

Subconsciously she rubbed the scarred welts on her face left behind from the slash of the knife that had been wielded out of drunkenness and anger. It was almost as though it had become second nature to try and smooth out the scars. Perhaps somewhere in the back of her mind she hoped the act would magically make the scars disappear.

Her constant companions: hate and anger, suddenly overwhelmed her and tears of frustration streamed down her face. She was so totally engrossed in her own little world of hurt and self-pity that she lost all track of time. When she finally composed herself it was dusk of early evening and the first stars of the night had been hung in the evening sky. She vaguely remembered Sarah calling her for the evening meal but, judging from the lateness of the hour, knew it was now too late to sup with them. She gave a little sigh as she descended from her comfortable hideaway to the room below. She must apologize to Sarah for her rudeness. Once inside, she found Jacob and Sarah in front of the hearth engrossed in their evening devotions. They looked up when she entered the room and gave her a smile. Jacob rose from his chair and motioned for Niccoli to sit down. "Please, come and join us," he invited.

"No! I find no reason to praise your God or mine," responded Niccoli. "Truly I mean no disrespect, please understand, but I am in no mood to pray to any God, yours nor mine." The memory of how the gods had deserted her when she most needed them was still etched quite vividly in her mind.

Niccoli watched from across the room as the light from the burning wood in the fireplace flickered upon the couple's silhouettes. She thought back to when the Hebrew couple had found her near death and, without question, had taken her into their home. Even though she could only remember bits and pieces of those first few days she did remember the feeling of love and compassion that had encircled her as she slipped in and out of consciousness. She knew that Sarah had been totally selfless during those first few days and had put her needs aside until her patient had passed her crisis. Sarah's actions, in the opinion of Niccoli, had truly displayed the meaning of unconditional love; to love without restraints and to love everyone as though they had the same value as she placed upon herself. That kind of love was rare and Niccoli had never experienced it before.

'If everyone practiced absolute love like Sarah and Jacob had displayed,' thought Niccoli, 'I would not be suffering from the injuries that were inflicted by the Roman soldiers that night in the alley," she said to herself. "It was because of their extreme selfishness that I now have to struggle with both physical and emotional scars. They, unlike Sarah and Jacob, had thought only of their pleasures without giving the slightest notice to my feelings or well-being. They treated me worse than they would treat any animal. What happened to me on that night was an act of violence completely opposite to the act of love and compassion that Jacob and Sarah have shown me.'

Niccoli focused back on the present. The sound of Jacob's prayers had a calming effect on her and before long she was peering through half-closed eyes as drowsiness overtook her. Soon Jacob's voice faded away and she fell into a most welcomed sleep.

When Jacob finished the evening meditation he rose and returned the Holy Scriptures and ceremonial garb to their proper places. He was staunch in his beliefs and looked after his sacred items with loving care.

"It has been a long day, Sarah, are you ready to retire?" he asked when finished. She did not respond to him and he turned his focus upon why she was so quiet. "Is there something wrong? You seem to be off in the distance somewhere," he added.

"Well, I was just thinking of Niccoli," Sarah finally responded. "When I look at her I see nothing but pain and frustration. It is obvious she is keeping so much bottled up inside her that needs to be released. She is so unhappy and it grieves my heart to watch her. Oh Jacob, her very spirit has been shattered, and I wish there was something more we could do for her. She needs to realize that she still has self-worth. What more can we do?"

Jacob himself had pondered over the same questions many times before. He knew they had helped Niccoli in every way that was physically possible but he was at a loss as to what else could be done to heal her inner pain.

"I don't know what more we can do for her," he replied. "Continued prayer is the only recourse that we have now. The Lord our God is the only one who can see deep into her heart and know exactly what needs to be done to have complete healing. Do you want to join together in a prayer to heal her spirit?"

"Yes," replied Sarah. She took her husband's hand and they knelt together before the hearth. They would do anything to make Niccoli whole again and a prayer vigil seemed but a small sacrifice to pay for a girl they had come to love. The one that filled the void they had always felt from never having a child of their own.

* * *

Try as she would, Niccoli could not escape the feeling of unrest. She felt torn between the safe haven of her friends' hospitality and the nagging whisper within her that was telling her to lay aside the tragic events of the past and continue forward. But how could she? She felt so ashamed. How could she face a world where she knew people would turn away because they could not bear the sight of her? How would she survive in a place where, in the short span of one isolated evening, she had been reduced to the state of a beggar? Something that was totally foreign to her. 'Perhaps,' she thought to herself, 'my first step would be to go back home. Penelope and Andros would be there to care for me.'

"Penelope and Andros!" Niccoli exclaimed out loud. "I have been so engrossed in my own hurts that I have not even thought of contacting them. How worried they must be. I must get in touch with them first thing tomorrow."

Her thoughts went back to Jacob and Sarah. She owed them her life and wondered how could she ever repay them for all they had done for her? She realized that words were so inadequate. How could she possibly show them how grateful she was? She knew that her friends were very proud people but perhaps they would accept something that had great meaning to her personally, like one of her Roman mementos. When she left for Jerusalem she had selected a few pieces of Roman art from her father's home that were very precious to her and brought them with her as visual reminders of her parents. Yes, one of them that would make the gift most meaningful and justly appropriate.

It would not be an easy task to tell her friends of her decision and hoped that she would be able to convince them that her leaving had nothing to do with the two of them. She had to make them understand that if she were to continue her healing, she could no longer depend upon them for her welfare. It was now time for her to resume that responsibility.

Once the decision was made, Niccoli felt as though a tremendous weight had been lifted from her shoulders. She was at peace with herself for the first time since the tragic events of that fateful night had occurred. Yes, she was scared and nervous about going out on her own but deep within herself she knew it was the only choice she had. By the time morning dawned, her mind was filled with all the things she planned to do. Now, instead of dreading to tell her friends of her decision, she was anxious to share the good news with them.

She hurriedly dressed and rushed down the stairs. Her face was flushed with excitement when she burst into the room below. "Oh, I am so happy," she exclaimed, her voice pitched high with excitement. She took Sarah by her hands and gleefully spun around in circles with her. For the first time since her ordeal she was dancing again. Together they maneuvered around the furniture in the small room until they were exhausted. They fell into the chairs beside the table and fanned themselves until they had cooled down and could catch their breath again.

"My goodness, Niccoli!" laughed Sarah, "Why are you

so joyous?"

"I have made a decision," she gasped in response to the inquisitive look on Sarah's face, "and I feel so good about it."

"Well, pray tell us about this wonderful decision?" said Jacob. He had heard the excited chatter and occasional bumping of furniture and had rushed into the room to investigate.

He listened intently as the words came tumbling out of Niccoli's mouth. It distressed him to hear of her decision to leave, but he decided to hear her out before starting his rebuttal. It seemed an eternity before she finally fell silent.

"Niccoli," he said, trying to keep his voice as calm as possible, "you are the daughter we never had and we do not want to lose you. I can provide for both you and Sarah. There is no need for you to go. Please, just give us a chance to help you work things out. We can surely find another solution that will be pleasing to all and yet be an outlet for your independence."

"Oh, I wish I could stay," said Niccoli. Tears came to her eyes as she looked at her loved ones. "You have both loved me without question, and I could never forget that I owe my life to you. I will forever be grateful to you, but I must find a place for myself." She hated the fact her friends would be hurt by her decision.

Jacob looked at Niccoli and felt great pride in what she was attempting to do, but he was troubled about how others would accept and treat her. "What will you do?" he finally asked. The concern that he felt was quite evident in his voice. In his mind he could not envision how a crippled girl could provide for herself.

"I don't know yet," Niccoli responded. "Perhaps Mary will allow me to help teach her students again, and if she will not allow me that pleasure perhaps she will let me mop the practice floor. At least that way I will be close to the dancing that I love."

She looked at her friends and could see the concern etched in their faces. For a long moment they stood looking at each other, feeling the strong bond that united them with more intense emotion than ever before.

Niccoli was the first to break the silence. "I love you so very much," she whispered. "I will never be lost to you. I promise that I will return often to visit you."

Before Sarah or Jacob had a chance to say anything else she gave each an embrace and then placed the veil over her face to conceal her scars, turned and walked through the doorway into the bright sunshine of a new and beautiful day.

"Well," Jacob said quietly to his wife, "it seems that Niccoli is determined to do things without our help."

"Yes, the house will certainly be quiet without her," Sarah replied and wished the feeling of emptiness that was in the pit of her stomach would go away.

Jacob took Sarah's hand and watched from the doorway as Niccoli turned for the last time to wave her goodbye. Her leaving was not what he or Sarah wanted, nor what they had asked for during their all night prayer vigil. It was times like this that he wanted to question God's wisdom. However, he knew that he had to put his trust in Him; knowing that He was looking after Niccoli and would know what was best for her.

* * *

Niccoli, anxious to return to the simple clay house she had called home since her arrival in Jerusalem, hurriedly made her way through the narrow dusty streets. She had not realized until now just how much she had missed it and longed to see the faces of Andros and Penelope. They were the closest link she had to her Roman family, and she wondered if they would be as happy to see her as she would be to see them.

At last, there in the distance...home! What a wonderful

sight! She broke into a run, but in her eagerness it seemed as though her feet were not advancing and she was moving in slow motion.

She was about to put her hand on the door latch when it opened without her touch. There, looming before her was a big burly man. His hair stood out in all directions and his clothes were heavily soiled. The sight of him was repulsive to Niccoli and she immediately jumped back.

Startled, the man fought to balance himself after stopping so abruptly from the surprise of Niccoli's presence. He spouted out a few choice profanities before he gained control and growled, "What do you think you are doing?"

"Who are you?" Niccoli snapped back. "Why are you in my home?"

"Oh, please forgive me," he replied, "but this is my home. The question is… who are you?"

"I am Niccoli, daughter of Roman Senator Cornelius Cademus," Niccoli huffed. "This is my home and it is obvious that you have invaded my property. I order you to step aside or I shall tell my father of your transgressions." Niccoli's face flushed with anger. How dare he think that he could invade her home.

"Oh, you frighten me!" the obnoxious man jeered. "Where is this father of yours? I see him not." As he spoke he waved his arm in a wide sweeping motion to indicate the area was void of anyone resembling a father.

His degrading attitude angered Niccoli even more, but she chose to ignore it. Why had Andros allowed this unpleasant man in her home? Where was he anyway?

"Step aside!" she ordered. "Tell my servants of my arrival."

"Step aside," he mocked. "Tell my servants I have arrived?" He was beginning to become more than a little agitated with this woman who appeared out of nowhere and accused him of stealing her home, even though he did take advantage of the fact that it was empty. To prevent Niccoli's entrance, he put his hands on both sides of the door jam and totally blocked the doorway.

"Why are you hiding behind that veil?" he asked as he boldly grabbed at it. "I want to talk with you, face to face."

Niccoli was quick to respond and warded off his aggression. "How dare you touch me or my veil," she uttered sharply and stormed past him into the house. "My father will put your eyeballs on the end of a stick and cook them over an open fire! How dare you prevent me from...." her voice trailed off as she stared at the unfamiliar furnishings. Where were her Roman mementos? And her servants; where were her servants?

"Where are my servants?" she demanded. "What have you done with my possessions?" The questions were directed more as statements of confusion than to the horrible man standing before her. "Andros...Penelope?" she called out. "Come forth," but there was no response.

The stranger, extremely angry by now, wanted this woman out of his house. "Leave this place!" he demanded in a booming voice. "You are not welcome here!" He was tired of bickering with her and grabbed her by the shoulders and forcibly shoved her out the door. The thrust was so great that it caused Niccoli to stumble and fall to the ground.

He stood for a long moment glaring at her, furious with her for disturbing his privacy. But his anger turned to laughter when he took notice of how she was sprawled in a most undignified manner in the middle of the street. His laughter was the disgusting kind that starts from the pit of the stomach and rolls out in thunderous ridicule.

"You are a crazy woman!" he gasped as he bent over double in an effort to catch his breath. He could not remember when he had enjoyed anything any more.

Niccoli scampered to her feet, stumbling at first in her haste to get away from the beastly man. She was stricken with disbelief. The hot sting of tears burned her cheeks as she fled aimlessly through the streets. She was unaware that she had wandered into the market place until she stumbled over some water jugs that a merchant had displayed outside his tent. They scattered in all directions and the sound of them bumping and clanking against each other was so loud that it jolted her awareness. She was afraid that they would all break into small pieces and scurried about to prevent them from rolling against each other.

"Watch where you are going!" shrieked the merchant. "Break one and you will pay for it!" He doubled up his fist and shook it at her in angry disapproval.

Niccoli reeled back, her eyes wide with shock as she looked at his angry face. She knew immediately that she wanted to get as far away as possible from him and his wares. Long after she had fled from his tent she could hear his yelling at her.

She ran for what seemed an eternity before she sank to the ground in total exhaustion. Her shoulders drooped in despair, and she felt so alone and abandoned. She started sobbing uncontrollably as she cried for the destruction of her dreams, for the loss of her hand and beauty, for the separation she felt from her mother, father and the ones who loved and cared for her. Most of all she feared for the uncertainty of what the future had in store for her.

She had started out with such hope and excitement. Then, without warning, everything went wrong. She had no home, no servants, nor any Roman mementoes to give to her dear friends. "Why?" she cried out between sobs. "Why me? What did I do that was so terrible to bring forth all of this punishment?" No answer came.

When she had calmed down enough to look about she realized that she did not recognize any of the surroundings. As a matter of fact, she did not even know from which direction she had fled, or how far she had gone. "Oh, great," she muttered to herself in disgust. "Now I'm lost. But then, why not? Why should anything be easy for me? I'm just an ugly crippled woman, I do not deserve anything better."

In the distance the sound of two young children talking excitedly to each other broke her concentration of self-pity. She looked up and saw them running in her direction.

"Hurry, my sister," the boy called to the younger girl who was running a few paces behind him, her little legs were moving as fast as they could to keep up with her brother. "I want you to see the Master who made my blind eyes to see." he continued. "We must get there before He departs."

In his excitement the boy was literally running circles around his sister. He wanted so desperately to again see the miracle worker, the man who had changed his life so completely, and the one whom he adored and loved because He had given him new hopes and dreams for the future.

Niccoli wondered what that boy was jabbering about? She was not aware of any Roman Gods that resided in Jerusalem. "Boy, wait," she called out, "Where is this Master of yours?"

"At the well," called the boy over his shoulder. He did not hesitate nor break his stride as he ran ahead. No one, especially a stranger, was going to slow him down.

Niccoli cupped her hands and called out again. "Where is this well you speak of?" But the boy and his sister were already far beyond hearing range.

She hurriedly gathered her belongings and ran to follow the two. If she could not catch up with them she hoped that she could at least keep them in her sight. Something deep inside was urging her to find out more about this 'Master' person. She did not understand the feeling, but knew that somehow, some way, she must see this man.

CHAPTER 6

Niccoli could not believe her eyes when she arrived at the well. There were people everywhere, some speaking excitedly to any one who would listen and others moving about quietly as they waited with great expectation for the man called Jesus. Then there were the curious; the ones who wanted to keep up with the latest craze.

Crippled and sick people, unable to arrive under their own strength, were being helped by friends or family. There were people lying on pads in the middle of the street and it seemed as though each time that she stepped over one person she found herself tripping over yet another. Everywhere she looked there were people lying, crouching, standing or leaning!

"He cometh!" yelled someone from the crowd. Immediately, as if by command, everyone pressed forward and demanded the attention of the man who was walking quietly in their midst.

"Heal me, Master!" yelled one.

"No, I was first!" yelled another.

The total chaos that enveloped the scene before Niccoli's eyes was very frightening to her. She watched as the stronger and healthier people shoved and elbowed their way through the crowd in an effort to get closer to this man who could heal by the touch of His hand. The sick and disabled were calling out for Him to heal them in one breath and in the next they were cursing the stronger ones for trampling upon them. It was a quagmire of hands waving for attention; accompanied by moaning, groaning and yelling. She had never experienced such an event before.

Just when Niccoli thought she could take no more of the confusion she felt a tug at her sleeve. She looked down to see a disfigured hand wrapped in dirty rags touching her. The areas of the hand not covered by the rags were snow white and crusty. Panic seized her and she immediately jerked her arm from the leper's grip. "Get away from me!" she screeched. "How dare you touch me!"

Niccoli looked at the spot where the leper had touched her. Why had she done that? Lepers knew it was unlawful to touch anyone. She started to run for the well to cleanse herself, but the leper grabbed her arm again. Niccoli glared back at the woman.

"Do you know the Master?" the leper asked, insistent to seek out help. "Won't you please speak for me?"

Niccoli noticed the soiled, oversized and tattered cloak that the woman clutched close to her body. She was a despicable sight that sent shivers down Niccoli's spine.

"Please help me," the leper pleaded.

Niccoli stepped back, afraid of being touched again.

"Do not turn away, I need your help," the woman pleaded. Something in her voice made Niccoli pause. She looked past her appearance and into her eyes. She could see desperation reflecting in them and for the first time Niccoli recognized the leper as a person like herself, not as some ugly beastly being.

Niccoli's heart went out to the doomed woman. As she looked at her she realized that she must have been very beautiful at one time, and suddenly she could identify with the unfortunate woman. She took note of how the woman crouched low, trying to avoid being noticed by others and her own fears melted into compassion.

Niccoli started to speak, but then noticed that the Master had raised His hand in a gesture to quiet the disorder. Almost immediately a hush fell over the crowd and they settled down to a peaceful murmur.

Niccoli was astounded. "What respect He commands," she whispered to herself. "He did not even speak a word and yet the multitude quiets."

The more she watched the miracle worker the more curious she became. How could a common man heal someone? Such a thing seemed quite impossible to her. In fact, it went against everything she had been taught. Things of that nature were only possible through her Roman Gods. But then, come to think of it, she had never seen her Roman Gods heal anyone either.

She strained on her tiptoes to raise herself above the others in an effort to see Him more clearly. Even though the multitude was pressing against Jesus to the point that she could hardly see Him, she concluded that He was a handsome man of medium height and strong stature. His shoulder length hair fell in soft waves about His face and His dress was simple, such as a commoner would wear.

He intrigued her and she watched closely as He lifted a crippled child and set her upon the well beside Him. He spoke ever so softly to her and the child listened intently. She never took her eyes off Him. As He spoke He massaged her leg and when He was confident that He had her full attention He gave her leg a quick tug. The small girl's eyes opened wide as she watched her leg immediately straighten. It was no longer a leg that would cause her to be different from other children.

He took her from her perch on the well's edge and stood her on the ground beside Him. She teetered at first and held tightly to His hand, afraid to take that first step. Jesus

patiently waited for her to gain confidence and then slowly, when she felt a little more secure, the child started placing one foot in front of the other. Soon she was squealing with delight as she ran from one person to another, showing them that she could run and jump like the other children.

Jesus stood back and laughed heartedly at the child's delight. It always pleased Him to see such joy in children. Then, lifting His gaze he focused once again upon the multitude. His eyes searched the crowd and came to rest upon Niccoli. He turned and made His way towards her.

Niccoli's heart skipped a beat. Surely He was not coming to heal her. She could see no logical reason why He should single her out among the many. He did not know her, nor could He see her scarred face behind the veil or the crippled hand she had tucked away in her sleeve.

While these thoughts were racing through her mind, Jesus stopped directly in front of her. She looked up at His face and immediately was lost within His eyes. Their gray blue color seemed to be liquid as tears of compassion and love glistened on their rims, and she felt a feeling of warmth and love flood over her. Never before had she felt so safe and secure as she did at this moment standing in His presence.

The Master lifted the veil away from her face and Niccoli froze with fear. She could not bear for anyone to see her disfigurement. She grabbed at the veil and pulled it back down over her face. In doing so she revealed her crippled hand. The feeling of being stripped naked consumed her. Not only had He exposed her face, but she had also shown her crippled hand.

'No, please don't,' she tried to scream out, but the words stuck in her throat and only silence followed. Her next impulse was to run away in shame but her feet were like heavy blocks of wood that would not respond.

"Niccoli," Jesus said in a soothing and comforting voice, **"it is alright."** He did not attempt to raise the veil again, but rather took her crippled hand from its hiding place and brought it up to His face. As He did so, a tear trickled down and moistened her fingers. He held it to His cheek for a long moment before He cupped it between both hands and then handed it back to her as though He was presenting her with a gift. He smiled and opened His hands to reveal a perfect hand. **"I return this to you,"** He said. **"It is healed and again whole."**

Instantly, Niccoli felt a tingling sensation as the feeling began to surge through her hand. She inspected her fingers and could see that they were now straight and perfect. She moved them and found there was no restriction whatsoever. She looked up and searched His face for an explanation of what had just happened, but He said nothing in response. Instead, He lifted her veil and took her face in His hands, bent down to make sure that He had her full attention and looked into her eyes. Niccoli felt as though He was looking into the depths of her soul. Even though it frightened her, she could do nothing but stand in awe of what was happening.

He gave her a reassuring smile and at that instant Niccoli knew that He understood her heartache and violation. Overcome with emotion she started sobbing uncontrollably. He took her into His arms to comfort her and immediately a feeling of security flooded over her. She began to relax and felt as though nothing could ever hurt her again.

Jesus held her until she was again able to gain control. She felt embarrassment for what she considered inappropriate behavior, but Jesus only smiled at her and gently kissed her on the forehead. Instantly she felt the same tingling sensation move across her face and upper body, the scars and familiar ridges on her cheeks melted away. Her face was again smooth and free of scars.

What words could express the gratitude she was feeling at this very moment? How could she verbalize how she felt? Not knowing what else to do she fell to her knees and

kissed His feet.

As she knelt before Him she felt His hand upon her shoulder urging her to rise. **"Niccoli,"** He said in a voice that was so gentle but yet seemed to resound from the heavens; **"rise and dance into the hearts of mankind so that they may know of the miracle that has happened here today in my Father's name."** He gave her a farewell smile, turned and was soon lost in the crowd.

Niccoli stood in disbelief. How had He known her name? And He knew she loved to dance! What had made her more special than the rest? Why had He chosen to heal her? She looked down at her hand and again moved her fingers. Yes, they were still operable. She touched her cheeks and found the flesh had remained soft and perfectly smooth. It was indeed true! The Master had just healed her!

Suddenly she remembered the leper. "The leper!" she called out. Jesus was already quite a distance from her. She jumped up and down, waving her arms in an effort to attract His attention. "Master, please heal the leper."

Jesus turned and smiled at her as he nodded his head.

"Thank you," replied Niccoli, "thank you." The full realization of what had just occurred overwhelmed her. She was healed!

She did not understand it, but she knew she wanted to share it with Jacob and Sarah. She wondered if she could find her way home after she had earlier ran so blindly through the unfamiliar streets, but she was surprised when she recognized things along the way and was able to retrace her steps. It was not long before she was bursting into their house and jabbering uncontrollably.

Jacob, startled at the sudden intrusion, looked up to see the maniac stranger raving wildly and talking in senseless disjointed sentences. "Who are you?" he interrupted. There was no sign of recognition in either his voice or eyes as he waited for an answer.

Niccoli was stunned. She did not understand his indifference and felt hurt that he did not welcome her with open arms. What was wrong? Had he forgotten her so quickly? Perhaps the love he had shown her before had only been a pretense. Then it hit her! Of course, he did not recognize her because he had never seen her with anything but a scarred face. How different she must look to him now.

"Jacob, it is I!" Niccoli laughed as she spun herself around so that he could get a better view of her. "The Master healed me today. Oh, Jacob, do you not understand me? The Master healed me!"

Jacob stood dumbfounded with his mouth hanging open, too shocked to utter a word or move a muscle. All he could do was stare at the beautiful woman standing before him. He had heard of the Master's healings and believed such things were happening, but he had never been witness to one. Now, he could see the results of a miracle standing before him. It seemed so unreal, almost more than he could accept.

Niccoli laughed gleefully and gave the mute Jacob a hug. She could identify with his difficulty to grasp the situation. She could hardly believe it herself.

"Niccoli," he whispered unbelievingly, "is it truly you?"

"Yes, it is I," she replied excitedly.

They stood looking at each other for a long moment, each feeling the magnitude of the events that had led up to this point. The joy that radiated from Niccoli's face reflected the hope she felt for the new life that had just been bestowed upon her. Yes, there was no doubt; a miracle had occurred.

"Sarah!" Jacob called out, suddenly remembering her. "Come, come quickly!"

Sarah, busy weeding her herbal garden, was oblivious to what was happening and the tone of Jacob's voice startled her. It rang of urgency as it pierced the silence of the garden. What was wrong?

"What is it?" she breathlessly asked as she sprang to her

feet. She did not take the time to rinse the dirt from her hands but rather wiped them on her skirt as she hurried to her husband's side. "What has happened?"

Jacob nudged Niccoli forward so that Sarah could get a better look at her. He chuckled as he watched her reaction change from that of anxiety to curiosity.

"Do I know this woman?" she whispered to her husband, trying to be as discreet as possible. She felt as though she should know her but, to the best of her recollection, she had never seen her before.

"You know her very well," Jacob assured her. "You do not recognize her because the Master healed her today." He paused for a moment to allow Sarah to grasp what he had just said before he continued. "Sarah, it is Niccoli!"

"No!" Sarah gasped, "It can not be!" She shook her head in disbelief as she looked at Niccoli; studying her face and then her slender body. It was only when Niccoli giggled and placed her hand upon her mouth in embarrassment did Sarah recognize the gesture. "Niccoli, it is you!" Sarah cried. "Praise be to God! Our prayers have been answered." She threw her arms around Niccoli and squeezed her with all the love she could express. "Please sit down and tell us all about it."

Sarah and Jacob listened as Niccoli explained every detail. She told them about the young boy and his sister, the crippled child at the well, and finally how Jesus had chosen her out of the many to be healed on that day; a day that had started out so disastrous but then, because of Jesus, had turned into the most joyous day she had ever experienced.

"Jesus has truly blessed you," Jacob responded when Niccoli had finished. "He must be the son of God! Who else could be capable of performing such a miracle? He has such love and compassion. Didn't you say He cried for you?" Jacob watched for Niccoli's response, he wanted to make sure that she understood the full impact of what had happened to her.

"Yes, he cried for me."

"Did Jesus say that it was His Father that healed you? Are you willing to put aside your Roman Gods for the deity of one? The one true God, the Father of Jesus?"

Niccoli thought about what Jacob had said and realized that she had been so excited about her healing that she had not thought about what it meant to have Jesus heal her. Yes, she had another chance in life; but now she also realized that her healing was from the one true God and Jesus wanted her to tell others of what He had done.

"Jacob, I will give up my Roman gods for the God of Jesus," she responded. "He is a mighty God and deserving of my loyalty and praise."

"Glory be to God!" Jacob shouted and threw his arms around Niccoli. He looked at Sarah and drew her into the hug also and the three reveled in God's glory together. It was truly a day for celebration and rejoicing.

Niccoli spent the night talking and planning with her friends. She could hardly wait for the morning to arrive so that she could hurry back to Mary's and continue with her studies. Thanks to Jesus, she was on her way to regain her status as a dancer.

CHAPTER 7

M ary was busy cleaning the classroom and preparing for her first class of the morning when Niccoli arrived. She felt agitated that a student would arrive so early and deliberately did not look up when the door opened. Wasn't it enough that she had to put up with the stumbling awkward youth all day! Why did she have to tolerate one of them earlier than need be?

"Mary," Niccoli said softly, sensing her teacher's irritation.

Mary stopped sweeping and tapped her broom on the floor, ready to scold her student for interrupting. Her irritation changed to surprise, however, when she realized it was Niccoli standing in the doorway. "Niccoli! Where have you been?" she cried out abruptly. She could not believe her eyes. Standing before her was the walking dead. "Your father searched Jerusalem twice over for you! When he could not find you we thought you were dead!"

"Is he here now?" Niccoli cried hopefully. She ached to see them and be comforted by them.

"Of course not. He couldn't find you," Mary continued. "He returned to Rome weeks ago. Andros had sent word to him that you had disappeared, but by the time he arrived both Andros and Penelope had vanished. Afraid of what your father might do, I suspect. And you, what an ungrateful daughter you are!" Mary scolded, as only a teacher can do. "Why didn't you tell us of your whereabouts?"

"So that was the reason for Andros' and Penelope's disappearance; allowing that ugly disgusting man to take over my home," Niccoli muttered aloud. "Father must not have gotten my message. I will send another one immediately."

"What did you say?" Mary's voice seemed harsh and demanding. It always irritated her when her students mumbled. "Oh, never mind," she continued. "I want to know where you have been all of this time."

Niccoli knew Mary was aching of curiosity to know the reason for her disappearance, but she was also confident she would not believe, or understand, the Master's healing. At this time she felt no need to go into detail about the events of the past few months. "I was taken very ill," Niccoli replied simply. "Strangers, who are now dear friends, took me into their home and nursed me back to health. I feel wonderful now and have returned to resume my lessons," she affirmed. "That is, if you will allow me that privilege."

Niccoli's short explanation was not enough to satisfy Mary's curious mind and she studied her student for a long moment. She knew that Niccoli was not telling her everything but then, why should she care about Niccoli's problems? Trying to keep the school open and teaching dense children simple routines was enough to keep her busy without worrying about another's problems. She turned her thoughts back to Niccoli's question, "Of course, you can continue your studies," she responded in her most pleasant voice. "Show me just how much you have remembered about your last dance routine."

By all outward appearances Mary was being very generous by allowing Niccoli to continue but, if the real truth was revealed, the only reason for her charity was because she did not want to lose the income or the connections that Cornelius had afforded her. She knew that he would do anything to please his daughter, and it was her plan to use his love for Niccoli to her advantage.

Niccoli was grateful to be back to her dance and spent every waking minute in the classroom. Even though she was quite busy she never forgot about her experience with Jesus, and still marveled at her healing. She thirsted for any additional information concerning Him, and was always curious to know where He was and what miracles He had performed. The more she learned of Him the more she wanted to know.

This day was no different. Jesus was on her mind as she hurried to the community well to draw her daily water. When she arrived she recognized a familiar face drinking from the cup that always hung dangling from a post nearby. She had never met him but had often seen him in the crowds that had gathered to listen to the Master's teachings. She thought he was rather handsome and her curiosity was peaked.

He did not see her approach and after he had quenched his thirst he gave a quick snap of the wrist to fling the remaining water from the cup. The water landed on Niccoli, and her cry of surprise at the sudden dousing made him aware of her presence for the first time. "Oh, please forgive me!" he apologized. "That was very foolish of me. Are you alright?"

"Yes, I am fine, but you certainly did startle me," Niccoli responded, laughing at the unexpected dousing. "I just was not expecting to bathe again so soon." She tried to shake the water off her dress, but it had quickly soaked into the fabric.

He started to dab at the water stain in an awkward attempt to help, but then refrained, too embarrassed and afraid Niccoli would be offended if he touched her.

Niccoli looked up at him and when their eyes met they both broke out in laughter.

"My name is Andrew. What might yours be?" he inquired when he had composed himself.

"Niccoli," she replied. "And now, if you will please

excuse me, I must draw my water and return home."

"Allow me to help you. It is the least I can do," he said and took the water jug from her hands. He not only wanted to assist her, but he also wanted to keep her attention as long as possible. "Haven't I seen you at the gatherings when the Master teaches?" he asked and then blushed when he noticed Niccoli's quizzical look. "I am sorry if I was offensive, but such a beautiful person as you is always remembered. I have often wondered who you were."

Niccoli blushed and turned her head.

"Oh my, I did it again. I am sorry," he apologized. "I did not mean to make you feel uncomfortable." The nervous laugh that followed only added to his charm. "It seems as though my actions are such that I am continually apologizing. May I make up for it by carrying your water home for you?" Andrew hoped the gesture would make amends for his stupidity. Besides, it would allow him more time to get to know her.

"You may," replied Niccoli, "but only if you tell me more about the Master. What do you know of him?"

"I know that He is a very gentle, loving man. His teachings do differ in some ways, however, from our Hebrew scriptures. For instance, our Jewish ancestors taught us that justice was an eye for an eye, but He tells us that we should love our enemies in the same way as we love ourselves," Andrew explained.

"I don't know if I can do that," Niccoli interjected.

Andrew smiled at her and asked, "Did you know that He was a carpenter's son and was born in a stable in Bethlehem? His parents had gone there to pay taxes and could not find a place to stay. I guess the stable was the only shelter. Mary, his mother, was a virgin, and Joseph, the carpenter, took her to wed despite the fact she was with child. He said an angel had appeared to him earlier and told him that the presence of God was with Mary, and that it was alright for him to take her as his wife."

"I have never heard of a virgin birth before," pondered Niccoli, "are you sure?"

"Yes, I am quite sure!" responded Andrew. "He, Jesus, is the son of the only living God."

Astounded at that answer Niccoli repeated, "The son of a God?"

"Yes, the only true God," said Andrew. He was intrigued with Niccoli's reactions as he talked. He thought that she was the most gorgeous creature he had ever seen, and was pleased with her interest in Jesus. It gave them something in common to talk about.

"You will have to explain more about the only one true God. In Rome we have many Gods. We have arrived at my home. Thank you for carrying my water," Niccoli said shyly, flattered by his attention.

"Will I see you again?" asked Andrew.

"I am sure we will see each other at the Master's gatherings," she replied and disappeared inside the modest home.

Andrew stood looking at the door that had closed behind her and hoped that she did not think him too much of a fool. But it did not really matter to him that it had been under such awkward circumstances because it had given him the opportunity to talk with her. She was undoubtedly the most beautiful woman that he has ever seen and he wanted desperately to be able to see her again, or, even better, ask her to stroll in the evening moonlight.

The Lord certainly has a funny sense of humor; he mused and wondered if Niccoli felt the same spark that he was now feeling deep inside.

* * *

The more Niccoli learned about Jesus, the more confused she became. She found it hard to believe that He was a carpenter's son as Andrew had told her. It made no sense to her at all. How could He be the Son of God if He was the son of a common laborer? She also had heard people say that He would be King someday. If that would come to pass, what would happen to her father's position as a Roman senator? For that matter, it would be quite possible that his very life would be in jeopardy. She knew what had happened in the past when kingdoms were taken over; people of authority were either killed or driven from their homeland. But Jesus was so kind and gentle, unlike any ruler that she had ever known. He simply did not fit into the mold of a typical king, so she had to know more.

Questions were still jumbled in her mind when she arrived at school the next morning. She quietly took off her dusty sandals and slipped into the strapped ones she used for dancing. She had just buckled the last strap when Mary finished her beginner's class and collapsed on the bench beside her.

"These students make me very weary," she complained. "I will certainly be glad when they can understand simple instructions. Happier yet when they can carry them out."

Niccoli looked up and smiled. She understood Mary much better now and did not always take everything she said seriously. "You love every moment of it," she teased.

Mary shot a sharp glance at Niccoli. How dare she defy me! However, when she thought about her student's observation she had to laugh. "Well, perhaps I enjoy it only a slight amount," she responded, and settled back on the bench with a smug look on her face. Yes, she was proud of her accomplishments and did love the attention it afforded her. "Oh, by the way," Mary continued, almost as an afterthought, "I heard that your Master is expected to be at the mountain today."

Niccoli's face lit up with excitement. "How wonderful! Who told you?"

"Just one of my many admirers," Mary responded flippantly. "It is beyond my belief how gullible you are about this man. He is just that, you know...a man. Nothing more, nothing less."

Mary rose and started walking to the practice area, directing instructions to Niccoli as she hurried along. "Now, let me see the results of your practice."

"Mary, wait," Niccoli interrupted as she rushed after her. "Come with me to the mountain."

Mary made a gesture, as if to say, 'don't bother me with such trivial matters,' and proceeded to ignore Niccoli's request.

"Mary, please go," Niccoli coaxed. "You have never seen the Master and it would mean so much to me."

Mary reeled about, her eyes flashing with anger. "Now, why should I care how much it means to you?" she blurted out. "I am a very busy woman and have no time to worry about pleasing you." Her voice was sharp, but when she started to turn away she hesitated and Niccoli could see her expression change to that of a scheming woman. "On second thought, maybe I will go," she said out loud, but she was thinking that after all He was a man, wasn't He? How could He possibly be a God, as some are saying? It might be interesting to see just how much of a man He really is.

"Alright, I will go with you, but just this once," she relented, concealing her thoughts from Niccoli. "You are my favorite student and, if it will please you, I will go."

Niccoli smiled. She knew Mary was not being honest with her, but it did not matter. What really mattered was that they were going to see Jesus. Mary tacked a quick note to the door, telling her other students that the classes would be canceled for the remainder of the day.

"Are you ready?" she asked Niccoli.

"More than ready," was the response.

The crowd had started to gather by the time they arrived at the mount. Niccoli looked around for Andrew and saw him seated with some friends on the hillside. She watched as he laughed lightly with the other man seated next to him, and then, almost as though he knew she was looking at him, he looked up and waved at her. She smiled and waved back. He took that as encouragement, excused himself from his friends and started over to her.

"I was watching for you," he admitted when he got within hearing distance of her, "and I was beginning to wonder if you were going to be here. I'm glad you finally made it."

"I was a little late in getting away from the dance studio," Niccoli answered and turned towards Mary and touched her on the shoulder. "Andrew, I would like you to meet my instructor; Mary, this is Andrew."

"I am very pleased to meet you," responded Andrew.

"As am I," replied Mary rather abruptly. "What do you know about this man called Jesus that Niccoli seems to think I should meet?"

"I think you are in for a treat," said Andrew. "The Master should be here shortly. Do you mind if I join you?"

"No, do whatever you want," snipped Mary, still not feeling comfortable about listening to a fanatical man.

"Do not mind her, she is nicer than she seems," laughed Niccoli. "She is used to being in control and is uncertain about coming here today."

"Oh, I see," chuckled Andrew, and then changed to a more serious tone. "Niccoli, not to necessarily change the subject but I have been meaning to ask you, how did you meet the Master?"

"It is a long story, but to make it short, I am one of the many that He has healed," replied Niccoli.

"You did not tell me," said Andrew, his curiosity peaked.

"You did not ask me," Niccoli replied, but her thoughts were on the day that she had been healed and remembered what Jesus had said: 'Go, dance into the hearts of mankind so that they might know of the miracle that has happened

here today in the name of My Father.' She gasped as the realization of what he had said started to take form. Today would be the perfect time for her to share her experience and demonstrate the love and gratitude she felt for Jesus. Dare she do it? Would He mind if she danced before the crowd that had gathered for Him? But, He did tell her to dance.

The more she thought about it the more her heart raced. At one point it beat so hard that she thought it would pound out of her chest. Yes, she had to do it. If she didn't, she was not sure but what she would die right on the spot upon which she stood.

Andrew was watching her and wondering what she was thinking about, but he remained quiet, waiting until she broke the silence.

"Andrew, I must excuse myself now," she said, "but I will return." She turned and mumbled something to Mary and hesitated for a moment before heading for the spot were she thought Jesus would most likely be. It was not as though she had never danced before an audience that made her uncomfortable, because she had done that more times than she could remember, but she was reluctant to do so before this particular gathering. What would their reactions be? How would Jesus view it?

She looked out across the sea of faces, sighed a deep sigh and took the castanets from her belt. Standing on her tiptoes with her hands above her tilted head she started swaying from side to side. Soon she was dancing with movements so graceful and flowing that she instantly captivated the crowd with her grace and beauty.

Andrew was thrilled and was so proud that he knew her. He wanted to get closer and looked at Mary to see if she would like to go with him but she stood rooted to the spot, dumfounded by what was going on. What did Niccoli think she was doing? She could not believe her eyes as she watched Niccoli weave in and out among the people. Every step and movement was perfectly executed. Never before had she seen her student dance so beautifully.

The crowd was so hushed when Niccoli finished that she thought they did not approve of her performance. Suddenly they all started cheering and clapping, and some even threw coins at her feet. She smiled a thank you, then hurriedly picked up the coins and tucked them away.

"Weren't you the one at the well?" yelled someone in the crowd who had recognized her. "Didn't Jesus heal your crippled hand and scarred face?"

Niccoli smiled and nodded. Soon the multitude was buzzing with the story of yet another miracle.

In all the commotion Niccoli did not notice a Roman soldier standing at the edge of the crowd. All the color had drained from his face, as though he had just seen a ghost. He thought she was dead. Panic started to set in because he knew of Cornelius and his search for his daughter. Had she told him about that night in the alley? Was he now a sought after man?

He could not risk Niccoli recognizing him, so he quickly turned his back to her and very discretely lost himself in the multitude of people. His only thought was to head for another part of town. It did not matter where, just so it took him as far away from Niccoli as possible. He could not take the chance that Cornelius would ever associate him with that incident in the alley. If he did, Marcos knew he would not be long for this world.

Meanwhile, Mary listened to what the people were saying about Niccoli. So that was the reason she had been absent for so long, but what had happened to cause her to be scarred and crippled? She was now certainly as beautiful and flawless as when she had disappeared. Mary's curiosity peaked to an ultimate high as she began to understand why Niccoli was so interested in this man called Jesus.

She looked around for Andrew, perhaps he could help solve

the mystery but she saw that he was already down the hill talking with Niccoli. She hurriedly made her way towards them. "Why didn't you tell me of this?" she asked when she got to Niccoli's side. Her voice was almost demanding as she quizzed her student. "Haven't I befriended you? Didn't you trust me?"

Niccoli was about to explain when a cheer rose from the crowd, and she looked about to see Jesus approaching the spot where she had just danced. "Oh, Mary, there He is now. Isn't He marvelous? See Him blessing the people as He draws near." Niccoli stood on her tiptoes so that she could see above the crowd. "Look!" she cried excitedly, "just look at Him!"

Mary needed no coaxing to look at Jesus. She could not take her eyes off of Him. He was one of the most handsome men she had ever seen, and she had known many, and He intrigued her with the gentle way He reacted to the people about Him.

The man beside Jesus was not someone she would easily forget either. He was handsome in a strong rugged way and she could see the bulging muscles in his arms as he raised them to quiet the multitude. In her mind He was an extraordinary man.

"I am Peter," he announced after the multitude had settled down, "and I would like to tell you a story about how Andrew, my brother, and I met Jesus. We were fishing in the Sea of Galilee and casting our nets into the sea with our partners, James and John. Neither of us had caught anything all day and we had brought our ships in to dock. We were busy washing and mending our nets when Jesus approached. There was a large group of people following Him and He asked if we would take Him out in the ship just far enough off shore so that the water would amplify His words; enabling the multitude to better hear Him."

"I did as He asked. When He completed His teaching He

told me to launch out into the deeper waters and let our nets down. I explained to Him that we had toiled all night and had not caught one fish, but He insisted that we go out. I did as He asked, but only to please Him."

Peter stole a teasing glance at Jesus, who responded with a chuckle. "When we cast our net it was immediately so full of fish that it broke from the weight of them. I immediately called to our partners, James and John, to come help us. In no time at all both of our boats were filled to the point of sinking. It was all we could do to return to shore."

"After things settled down, Jesus spoke to us of things to come and when He was finished he simply said, 'Follow me and I will make you fishers of men.' Without hesitation, we laid down our nets and have followed Him ever since. It has been a wonderful year. I have seen miracles beyond my belief or understanding. His teachings and interpretations of the scriptures are in many ways different from the way I was taught to believe. He teaches of love and understanding, not revenge. He tells us that the old way of believing 'an eye for an eye' is no longer the way that the Lord wants for us to act. Jesus tells us to love each of our enemies as ourselves and to do good to those that treat us badly. That is hard to do because when we are hurt we want to seek revenge. But He says that vengeance is for the Lord."

"I have known no other man like Him. For me, I would follow Him to death but you must choose for yourself. All I ask of you is to listen with open hearts and ears...thank you for coming," Peter said as he concluded his speech. He sat down beside Jesus to wait, along with the multitude, for Him to speak. There was a hushed silence as everyone waited in anticipation for the wisdom that this great Master would soon reveal.

CHAPTER 8

J esus rose from the rock upon which he was seated and
smiled at the hushed crowd before Him. After a brief
pause He spoke in a loud, clear voice so that all could hear.
"Love thy neighbor as thyself," he stated.

"Who is thy neighbor?" someone yelled from the crowd.

Jesus knew the man to be a lawyer and understood that his
intent was to discredit Him. He did not, however, allow it to
provoke Him. **"To better understand I will tell you a
story,"** he replied in a calm but confident manner.

**"A certain man was going from Jerusalem to Jericho
when he fell among thieves. They stripped him of his
clothing and wounded him, leaving him half dead in
a ditch.**

**A priest, a holy man, happened to come along the way
and saw the wounded man but, not wanting to risk possible contamination, went to the far side of the road;
leaving the injured to die. Later a Levite, whose function
is to assist the priest and serve the congregation, passed
by and also ignored the injured man. It was not until
later that a Samaritan, a social outcast who traditionally
had hostility for the Jews, had enough compassion for
the man to stop and help him.**

He first poured wine and then oil over the man's wounds and bound them to stop the bleeding. When he had finished he put him upon his ass and took him to the nearest inn where he sat up with him all night until the crisis passed. The next morning he gave the innkeeper two denarii and told him to continue caring for the victim until he could return and pay him for any additional expenses.

Now, which of these three travelers was a neighbor to the man who fell among thieves?"

"The Samaritan," was the response from the crowd.

"Go and do likewise," Jesus instructed and then dismissed them with a blessing.

Niccoli's thoughts went to Jacob and Sarah. They truly had been neighbors to her when they had found her on the threshold of death, lying slashed and bleeding in the alley. Without hesitation they had taken her into their home and sat by her bed both night and day until she was well again. The love they had bestowed upon her showed no bounds. Yes, they were truly examples of what Jesus was explaining to the multitude today when He said, 'Love thy neighbor as thyself.'

The crowd started to disperse and somehow Mary was lost in the midst of it all. Niccoli looked for her, but soon gave up. There was something more important she wanted to do. For a long time she had wanted to do something for Jesus that would show her love and gratitude for all He had done for her, and now she knew what she could do. She hurriedly took the coins she had tucked away earlier and clutched them in her hand. It seemed like such a meager gift, but perhaps it would purchase a couple of loaves of bread for Him and His disciples.

She looked around to see where Jesus had gone and saw that He had not gotten far. As usual there was a crowd of people who had brought their crippled or ill children, friends, spouses or parents for Him to heal. She drew closer to the group in order to better see what was happening. As she watched Jesus speak to each individual, she could see the love that radiated from His being. She remembered how she felt when He healed her, and cried tears of joy for the people who were now recipients of that same love.

Not wanting to disturb Jesus, she searched for one of His disciples. Finally, she recognized a man who was standing at the edge of the gathering and headed in his direction. She did not know him by name, but knew he was one of the chosen twelve and she deduced that he was the caretaker of the money since he carried a money pouch strapped about his waist.

"Are you one of Jesus' chosen twelve?" she asked sheepishly.

"Yes, I am one of the chosen," he replied proudly.

"Would you please take these few coins in gratitude for what Jesus has done for me? It is but a small token, perhaps only enough to buy your supper," Niccoli apologized.

Judas smiled. "Bless you, my child," he said as he put the coins in his pouch.

Niccoli felt exhilarated! She had done something for the Master that was meaningful and fulfilling. She knew at that moment she had to follow Him wherever He might go and dance before the people as she had done today. She wanted more than anything else to be a living example of the love He displayed and taught.

A sense of satisfaction filled her. "Yes, I must let the people know how wonderful Jesus is, and I know of no other way to explain it than to show them how He healed my body and enabled me to dance again. I have been made whole because of Him and I want to share that blessing with others," she affirmed to herself.

Again, she turned her attention to searching for Mary, but the pressing crowd of people, and the chaos that they created, was beginning to be too much for Niccoli. She was about to give up and start for home when she caught a glimpse of Mary kneeling at the feet of Jesus, and she shoved her way through the crowd in time to hear Mary's question to Him.

"Where do I go from here, Lord?" Mary asked as she lifted her eyes upward to Jesus. She was jubilant about the forgiveness and compassion that Jesus had shown her but she was confused. Questions flooded her mind as she tried hard to discern her feelings about the events of the day.

"Do not be afraid Mary, just do one step at a time," Jesus affirmed, **"and learn to leave the negative behind you. Dwell on the perfect but understand the imperfect, both in yourself and others, and realize that perfection is always a constant reaching ahead.**

Understand that you are now one with me, and that everything is possible through me. I will help you to recognize illusion and understand truth, as the two often seem inseparable and can be very deceiving. Wisdom for that understanding is within your grasp; you need only to ask.

And remember, it is very important that you do not let your ego deceive you; it is the most common pitfall of all. Instead, lay yourself aside and share with others my ultimate love. For I say to you my child, that from this day forward and through eternity, we are united together in love."

Jesus helped Mary to her feet, excused Himself, and turned His attention to a crippled child. She stood in shock and pondered over what she had just experienced. Through His love and compassion, Jesus had cast out the devils that had been inhabitants of her body for so many years. The miracle of His blessing now enabled her to fully understand why Niccoli was so devoted to Him. He was truly a great man, and there was no doubt in her mind that He was the Son of God!

She also realized that she was a changed woman; gone were the desires to taunt men and use her body for personal gain. Now, the most important thing for her was to be a pupil of Jesus, and follow Him whenever and wherever she could.

"Mary!" Niccoli cried out as she ran up and grabbed her teacher's hands, "I heard what Jesus said to you! Oh Mary, how exciting! Now will you follow Him?"

In her excitement, Niccoli did not realize that she was squeezing Mary's fingers so hard that they ached. Mary winced and confirmed, "Yes, from this day forward, I will always devote my life to Him!"

"I am so happy! Words can not express how happy I feel," Niccoli replied, her voice was shrill from the excitement that she felt. She looked down and saw Mary rubbing her fingers, "Oh, I'm so sorry I hurt your fingers," she apologized, "I'm just so excited!"

"I know," Mary responded softly, "but they still hurt." She looked at Niccoli and recognized the fact that she was not only her student but also now her mentor. She could contain herself no longer, and threw her arms around Niccoli's neck and sobbed the tears of joy that only a new disciple of Jesus can understand.

From that day forward, Mary was no longer the rigid temperamental taskmaster who gave way to fits of temper. Niccoli was grateful, both for herself and for the sake of the other students, because there had been many times that Mary had made their studies very difficult. Studying under her now was most pleasurable, and it was not long before the two women became close friends.

"Niccoli, I have been thinking," Mary stated one evening after the last student had gone home, "what more can we do for Jesus and His chosen twelve?"

Niccoli had noticed earlier how quiet Mary had been and was very curious about her silence, but she was surprised at her question. "I do not know," she replied as she pondered over the question, "what are you considering?"

"Well, it seems to me that there would be a lot that we could do for them, such as preparing meals or washing their clothes."

"You do not think that it is enough to dance for the multitude while they wait for Jesus?" Niccoli hopefully asked, because she definitely did not think of herself as a servant.

Mary knew what her friend was thinking and she laughed before responding, "Niccoli, perhaps it is you who needs to be the servant."

"Mary, how can you say that? In what way would it help for me to be a servant? Please...I had to get used to washing my own clothes, now you want me to wash another person's dirty clothing?" Niccoli was quite serious; she had no intention of being anyone's servant.

"Just how bad can it be?" questioned Mary.

"Bad enough!" replied Niccoli.

"What a spoiled child you are," scolded Mary.

"Perhaps so, but that is a ridiculous idea!" declared Niccoli, and she shuddered at even the possibility of doing such a thing.

"You think about it," responded Mary. "I just know what I must do, however, if need be I can do it without your help. You must decide how you want to serve Jesus."

"Don't get so upset, I just have never done such a thing before."

"Then it is about time that you do," affirmed Mary as she silently laughed to herself. She knew that Niccoli would not want to be left out and, even though it would be a big adjustment for her, she would eventually give in to the proposal.

"Let us go home!" Mary suggested. "We have had a long day and I am very tired."

"It certainly sounds good to me," agreed Niccoli. "I have only a few more scarves to hang up, and then I will be ready." She was hanging up the last student's scarf when she heard a knock on the door. "Are you expecting anyone, Mary?" she asked.

"No, are you?" was the reply.

Niccoli shook her head and waited.

"Who is it?" Mary called out, and put her ear against the closed door so that she could hear the reply.

"It is I, Senator Cademus," was the answer.

Mary's eyes opened wide, had she heard correctly? Was it Senator Cademus, Niccoli's father? "What do you think Niccoli?" she questioned, "Is that indeed your father's voice?"

"Well, yes, I think so," Niccoli stuttered. Was it true? Was her father here?

"For goodness sake, don't you know your father's voice?" Mary blurted out. "Do I open the door or don't I?" she asked in her stern teacher's voice.

"Yes, yes, open the door!" Niccoli squealed with delight. There was no question. She was now confident that the voice she heard was indeed that of her father and she wanted desperately to see him, to feel the comfort of his arms around her.

Mary opened the door and revealed that not only was Cornelius there, but also Diana. Niccoli could hardly believe her eyes! At last they were standing before her.

"Mother! Father!" she shrieked as she ran towards them. "Oh, I am so glad to see you!" she gasped between hugs and kisses. "You look wonderful! It's been so long! How are you?"

Niccoli was so excited to see her parents, and wanted to make up for all the time that had lapsed since they were last together, that she quickly skipped from one question to another. Cornelius and Diana, not having enough time to respond between questions, silently watched and listened to their daughter.

"Didn't you get my first message telling you I was at Jacob

and Sarah's home? I could not find Andros and Penelope, did you send them away or did they return to Rome?"

"Calm down, calm down, my daughter," laughed Cornelius, "you are going much too fast for your mother and I to keep up with you."

"I apologize," chuckled Niccoli, "I am just so happy to see you."

"Well, for starters, who are Jacob and Sarah?" asked Diana.

"They are the ones that saved my life and nursed me back to health!" replied Niccoli.

"What do you mean? Nursed you back to health?" questioned Cornelius.

"It is a long story and I will tell you everything about it, but first I want you to meet them. I have been staying with them since that nasty man took my house."

"What nasty man. Did he hurt you?" asked Diana.

"No, no....Oh, let us not talk about it now. Come, I want you to meet Jacob and Sarah," Niccoli stated. "Mary, are you coming with us?"

"Not tonight, you have a lot to catch up on," replied Mary. "I will see you on the morrow. Cornelius and Diana, it was so nice to see you both again. I am so glad that it is under more pleasant circumstances this time. Shalom."

They bid Mary farewell and headed for the home of Jacob. Niccoli was jabbering constantly and it was hard for Cornelius and Diana to decipher what she was saying but they tried to piece together the jumbled mess the best that they could. The only thing that really mattered was that they were now walking beside their once lost daughter.

"This is their house. See how Sarah has planted flowers and herbs around the house. Aren't they pretty?" Niccoli asked with pride.

"Yes, yes, of course," Diana stammered. She was comparing the stark clay house to her marble one with beautiful manicured gardens, and in comparison she thought the flowers, herbs, and house were pitifully sick looking. But, in her usual gracious way she would never say it aloud, not even to her daughter who was so obviously impressed.

Niccoli opened the door and called out. "Sarah, Jacob, where are you? There is someone with me that I want you to meet." She took note of how the house was filled with the aroma of her favorite lamb stew and took a deep breath before continuing, "My, does it ever smell good in here. You have just made me realize how hungry I am."

Cornelius and Diana waited at the door and surveyed the meager furnishings, they were not sure that they wanted to enter.

"Please, Mother and Father, do not hesitate. Go in and have a seat next to the hearth," Niccoli encouraged.

"Are you sure? We did not inform them of our arrival," Diana stated, noting that etiquette was not being observed, but also searching for an excuse to not enter.

"Mother," Niccoli said and moved closer to her mother so that she could whisper in her ear, "Please, do not embarrass me, this is not Rome."

Sarah was putting the last of the herbs into the stew and had her back to the door when the guests arrived. "Niccoli, I was starting to worry about you," her voice showed the relief that she felt to have Niccoli home. "Who is it that you wish me to met? Is it that nice boy you met at the well?"

"No, it is not Andrew, why don't you turn around and see for yourself. Where is Jacob?" Niccoli asked.

"I sent him to the market place, he will return shortly," Sarah answered as she dried her hands and turned to greet Niccoli's guests. "Oh my," she gasped and her heart pounded at the sight of the two elegant Romans standing inside the doorway. She knew immediately that they were Niccoli's parents and her first thought was that they were going to take Niccoli back to Rome and she would never see her again. "You must be Niccoli's parents," she said when she was able to breathe evenly again.

"Yes, Cornelius and Diana," Cornelius said with a polite bow, "Niccoli has been telling us about how you have befriended her. We are forever grateful and in your debt."

"We love Niccoli, and want the very best for her, you owe us nothing," replied Sarah.

"You are most gracious," Diana affirmed, "we also want the best for Niccoli, so I am sure that you will agree with me that the best thing for her to do now is to return home with us. We have been separated for far too long! Don't you agree Niccoli?"

"Yes, Mother, I agree that we have been separated far too long," Niccoli responded but before she could say more she was interrupted by Cornelius.

"Good," he declared, "then it is settled! You will return with us on the morrow!"

"Father, let us talk this over," interjected Niccoli.

"What is there to talk over? It is settled!" replied Cornelius; making it appear as though it was a business decision.

Sarah looked first at Cornelius and then at Niccoli and could sense that an argument was about to occur. She wanted to avoid it if at all possible and suggested, "Please, join me for dinner at my humble table. I think I hear Jacob's whistle and he will arrive at any second. Let us first eat and when we are comfortable and relaxed we can then talk."

"Yes, that is a wonderful idea," agreed Niccoli. She would grasp at anything to avoid a confrontation with her father. "Sit here beside me Father, and Mother I would like for you to be on my other side. Both of you, please, sit down," Niccoli coaxed and patted the chairs beside her.

Cornelius huffed a little and reluctantly sat down. Diana followed her husband's lead and tried to cover his inexcusable behavior. "Whatever you have prepared it certainly smells delectable," she said with a smile.

Jacob entered the room and stopped abruptly when he saw

the Romans seated at his table. "Well, Sarah did not say we were having guests," he managed to say politely. "I am happy to be able to share my food with such honorable guests."

"Jacob, I am so glad you are here," Niccoli exclaimed, relieved to find another excuse to draw her parents' attention away from returning to Rome, "these are my parents, Cornelius and Diana."

"I am honored to have you as my guests," Jacob responded. "Niccoli has told us so much about you. For her sake I am very glad that you have arrived."

"Thank you for your hospitality," replied Cornelius, "and we are also glad to be here. When we received Niccoli's message that she was alive and well, we had to rush to her side. We were so worried that she had met with disaster and we would never see her again."

"Yes, Father, you might say that I did meet with disaster, but because of these two loving people I am here to speak with you today," said Niccoli and she decided that it was now the appropriate time to begin telling them the entire story of what had happened. Even though she knew that her father would be outraged that it was Jesus who had healed her, and not one of his Roman Gods, she made it a point to tell him every detail. An hour passed and, when she was finally finished, she tried to determine what her father's reaction was, but she could not read his face. She could not tell if he was angry, upset, or in disbelief with the fact that Jesus had healed her, so she waited quietly for his reaction.

Cornelius didn't even know how he felt. He wanted to yell, I told you so, Niccoli, but knew that was of no consequence now. He wanted to find the men that had done this to his daughter and tear them apart slowly and deliberately, he wanted to order her to go home with them so that he could keep a closer eye upon her, he wanted to hug her but at the same time spank her for insisting that she come to Jerusalem and he definitely wanted to meet this Jesus of her's because he could not believe that He could do such a healing. "Niccoli, I do not know what to say," he finally pointed out.

"I know," Niccoli responded.

"I am just glad that she is fine and well!" Diana interjected. "We have her here with us now, that is the only thing that really matters!"

"Yes, that is true Diana, but where do we go from here?" questioned Cornelius.

Diana gave him a helpless look and shrugged her shoulders. "I just want Niccoli safe," she responded.

Everyone was quiet and looked down at their hands, trying to avoid looking at one another. No one knew what to say and each wanted to avoid a confrontation, so the silence became very awkward.

Cornelius was the first to break the silence, "Niccoli, I think that the decision to stay or go back to Rome is yours alone. You may, of course, stay here with your friends whom I find to be very charming; or you can go back with your mother and me. You know that we love and miss you with all of our hearts, but I have wrestled with my very soul and have decided that your mother and I will abide with whatever decision you make; no matter how hard it might be for us to do so."

"Oh Father...." Niccoli sobbed.

Cornelius went over to Niccoli and placed his hand on her shoulder to comfort her, "Think about it tonight," he said in a gentle voice, "and give us an answer in the morning. Now, tell me, is there an inn close by that we might spend the night?"

"Please, you are our guests, I will prepare a place for you in the upper room." responded Jacob.

"That is very kind of you," thanked Diana, "It has been a long day and we are very tired." She glanced at her husband to see what his reaction was going to be in response to the offer of hospitality and, before he could make a response, she thanked Jacob and then turned to her daughter. "Niccoli, know that I love you," she said. "Have a good night's rest."

The night was long and seemed to never end as Niccoli tossed about in her bed. She thought over everything that her father had said, and remembered the pleading look that her mother had given her when she kissed her goodnight. "What should I do, dear Lord?" she asked, "I love my parents as I could love no others, but I also love You, my Saviour. I have turned my life over to You, and have promised to follow You until death." Then, with clarity of thought, the answer was there for her. She must stay in Jerusalem!

The next morning there was awkward silence between Cornelius and Niccoli as they sat with the others at breakfast. Niccoli hesitated to tell her father of her decision because she knew how much it would upset him, and Cornelius was hesitant to ask because he was afraid of hearing what his daughter's decision would be.

It was Diana who finally broke the silence. "Well, this quiet is more than I can endure," she said. "Won't someone say something?"

Niccoli looked at her father and then back down at her plate. She anticipated a long discussion and dreaded the thought of starting it but, when she looked up again and saw her father looking at her, she knew that the time had come for the confrontation. There was no easy way to say it so she just blurted it out, "Father, I have decided to stay in Jerusalem. I know that you are not going to agree, but I must stay and help Jesus with His work."

Cornelius laid his spoon down and pushed himself back from the table. She had just said the very words that he most dreaded hearing, but he remembered his promise from the night before and knew that he had no rebuttal. "I see," he said after a long hesitation. "There is nothing I can say to change your mind?"

"No, nothing, I have wrestled with this decision all night and I stand firmly behind it," replied Niccoli.

"Then I must find more servants for you." Cornelius declared. "I want someone that can help you and watch over you."

"But, Father, I am taking care of my own needs," Niccoli confirmed, "and Jacob and Sarah are here if I need help. They have always treated me as their own and watch over me with love, not duty."

"But they are not your servants! You need servants!" argued Cornelius.

"No, I do not!" argued Niccoli. "I have friends, I do not need servants!" Niccoli was firm in her statement, letting it be known that she strongly believed in what she was saying. "Jacob and Sarah," she continued, "have shown me how to care for myself, and I really do not mind doing my own wash and bath. In fact, I enjoy going to the market for Sarah and helping her bake bread."

"Niccoli, you and your mother are the only two people with whom I can never win an argument!" attested Cornelius as he threw his hands up in submission. "I will, however, find Andros and Penelope, and see that they get their just punishment for not protecting you from the injury and misery that you encountered. They will have to answer to me for what they have done."

"Please, Father, no! I do not wish any harm to come to them! It was my fault that I was alone that night, not theirs. The reason that Andros was not with me was because I had sent him home earlier; it was not because he had abandoned me. He never shirked his duty! He was always faithful and obeyed my every command. Let them go free, I am sure that fear of your wrath has made them suffer enough."

"Niccoli, let me understand. One, you do not want servants. Two, you do not want me to punish Andros or Penelope. Three, you want to stay in this God forsaken place and follow this Jesus, whomever he may be, and devote your life to Him," Cornelius verified.

Niccoli smiled at her father, "Yes," she said simply, "that is correct."

"I do not understand your reasoning! But I will give in to you as I said I would do. Your decision is firm?"

"Yes."

"Then it shall be so," Cornelius affirmed.

"Thank you, Father," replied Niccoli, "I promise to frequently keep in touch with you. Mother, I love you so, please do not worry about me."

"Niccoli, not being able to see you, or touch you, will always make me worry about you. Please, take care, and know that I love you!" Diana sobbed.

"Diana, there is nothing more we can do here. Let us be on our way," Cornelius said, chocking back the emotion that he felt. "I will see to it that you have enough money to live comfortably." He saw that Niccoli was about to protest and raised his hand to stop her. "At least allow me to help you in that way," he pleaded.

Niccoli nodded and gave her parents one last hug and then they were gone, leaving her with a lonely feeling that no one else would ever be able to fill.

CHAPTER 9

It was on a beautiful spring day about a year later; Jerusalem was bustling with the people who had come for the annual Passover and Mary and Niccoli found themselves caught up in the festivities of the event. They were walking to the market place when they saw two of Jesus' disciples, Philip and Bartholomew, leading a rather frisky and obviously untamed donkey.

"Philip! Bartholomew!" Niccoli called out and waved to get their attention as she ran to greet them. "Shalom! When did you get back? Does this mean that Jesus is also here?"

"Niccoli, please be careful, this donkey will kick you in the side of the head if you are not careful," Philip cautioned. "Yes, in answer to your question, Jesus will be here soon. We have come to get this donkey, or should I say wild demon, for Him to ride upon when He enters the city."

All the time that Philip was talking, the donkey was braying and kicking up his heels in protest to the rope that was tied around his neck. Everyone scattered when it got a sudden burst of energy and ran forward, pulling Philip along behind with his heels dug into the dirt. Bartholomew yelled and quickly grabbed the rope to help Philip and, with their combined strengths, they finally stopped the rebelling donkey.

"Why the Lord wants this particular donkey is beyond me," laughed Bartholomew when everything had quieted down. "That was quite a test of wills! I think we should hurry along before it happens again. Ladies, Shalom for now."

"Shalom," replied Mary, "see you soon."

Others had also seen the disciples and it had taken little time for the news of Jesus' return to spread throughout the community. The entire city was charged with excitement as people assembled at the entrance gate to greet Him. They had gathered palm leaves as a symbol of triumph and rejoicing and were waving them in the air while they sang songs of Hosanna in celebration of His arrival.

Mary and Niccoli hurried along with the others. They were aware of what had happened in Bethany only six days prior when Jesus had raised their friend Lazarus from the dead. They had heard that by the time Jesus had arrived at the tomb Lazarus had been dead for four days. Everybody had warned Him that the body would surely stink by now. But regardless of their warnings, Jesus called for Lazarus to come forth from the tomb. When he walked out he looked calm and refreshed as though he had only been sleeping. In Niccoli's estimation it was Jesus' greatest miracle and she could hardly wait to talk with Him about it.

Everywhere that Niccoli walked she could hear people talking about the miracle but, even though she felt the excitement all around her, she also sensed that something was terribly wrong. She discerned the people carefully and could not help but wonder whether many of them really loved Jesus as she did, or did they simply want to see the magic of a miracle worker. She watched the Pharisees huddle together and knew of the commandment they had recently issued stating that if any man knew where Jesus was staying they were to inform them immediately. She knew it was their intent to harass Him, and she couldn't help but worry about His safety. Wasn't He afraid of them? He had to know of the commandment, but after she thought about it she wondered why she was so worried; He was, after all, the Son of God! He could take care of Himself.

"Niccoli, there comes Jesus now!" Mary cried excitedly. "Look, He is riding the untamed donkey that we saw Philip and Bartholomew leading earlier. See how gentle it is now!"

The two women pushed ahead and got as close as possible to where Jesus would be passing. There were people everywhere; crowding, pushing, and laying palm branches down before Him. Some even placed their cloaks on the street for Him to ride over. Niccoli had never before seen such jubilation among the people.

As He rode past them Niccoli caught His eye and blew Him a kiss. He smiled in return and she could see no sign of worry on His face, which made her feel reassured. Just as she turned to run alongside of Jesus she bumped into a Pharisee who was standing nearby. "See, did I not tell you this would happen?" she heard him say to another standing beside him. "We have gained nothing. The whole countryside has turned toward Him. We must stop this trend immediately."

"Oh, I do hope Jesus knows what He is doing," Niccoli quietly whispered to herself as she watched the two hurry off together, totally engrossed in their devious plans. The day closed, however, with no harmful acts perpetrated against Jesus and Niccoli relaxed a bit. Be that as it may, she still prayed a prayer of protection for Him before she turned in for the night.

Unknown to Niccoli, her prayer would not be answered in the way she desired. Her desires were secondary to the importance of Christ's mission: to die upon a cross for the redemption of man's sins. Jesus was now carrying out what needed to be done to fulfill the scriptures.

She awakened to a beautiful morning and was full of anticipation for the new day. She lay in bed for a few moments to listen to the sounds of birds singing outside her window, 'What a glorious morning,' she thought to herself as she stretched and then snuggled back into the comfort of the cozy bed to plan the day ahead of her. She enjoyed being self-sufficient and had grown to love gardening and caring for her home. Preparing her own food had become a favorite hobby and she especially enjoyed sharing the overabundance with the poor. There was little doubt in Niccoli's mind that her father would be upset and totally unable to comprehend her strong desire to share the greater portion of her allowance on beggars and lepers.

But today she must concentrate on the Passover. Planning for it gave her a sense of belonging and provided her with a chance to see prior students and friends from neighboring villages. "First," she concluded, "I must bake the bread while the morning is still cool and then I will wash the Master's clothes." She looked out the window to see where the sun was and realized that she had to hurry if she was going to accomplish everything before noon. She jumped out of bed and hurriedly dressed as she hummed along with the songbird. What a glorious morning to do her chores.

She could feel the morning passing all too quickly and hurriedly folded the clothing that she had washed for her beloved Master and His disciples. She ran to get a couple of the freshly baked loaves of bread and placed them beside the neatly stacked laundry. She quickly surveyed the items and when she was satisfied that everything was there she gathered them into her arms and hurried out the door to head for the home that Jesus used whenever He and the disciples were in Jerusalem.

When she arrived, she peeked in the open doorway and saw Judas completely engrossed in balancing the ledger. She was surprised to see the amount of coins stacked before him and wondered who had been so generous.

"Shalom, Judas," she said cheerfully, "how are you today?"

Niccoli's voice startled Judas and when he looked up at

her his face flushed with embarrassment. He quickly gathered the coins from the table and put them into his pouch, "Shalom to you," he replied as he composed himself, "please, come in and rest. I had forgotten that you were coming. I regret that you have missed the others."

He noticed the inquisitive look on Niccoli's face and proceeded with an explanation. "You know, Niccoli, I try very hard to make sure there is enough money for our needs," he said. "I don't know if you are aware of it or not, but it takes quite a lot to support our ministry. I get so frustrated with Master. He never worries about money and says silly things such as 'Even the lilies of the field are clothed.' Well, that sounds so beautiful, but the harsh reality is that it takes Roman coins to feed and clothe us."

"He makes me so angry when He gives the money away! I must keep some hidden at all times, or we would have nothing at all. Sometimes I wonder about His capabilities. Where would we be if I had not watched over the money for Him?"

Niccoli watched Judas as he spoke and could see how upset he was. She knew in her heart that he was much too obsessed with his position as treasurer, and sensed it had become a priority over everything else. How could she answer his question in a way that would make him realize how much importance he was placing on money?

"I am sure Master knows what He is doing. You need not worry so much," she replied. She could see him flinch at that response and suddenly she felt very uncomfortable. "I must go, Judas, there is much I have to do before nightfall. Please give the others my love. Shalom, and don't worry so."

Judas only glanced her way in recognition of her departure, again too engrossed in his ledger. Niccoli wondered if Jesus had noticed how angry and greedy he had become.

Niccoli had no way of knowing that at this moment the scriptures were being fulfilled. The Priests, Elders, and Council had already charged Jesus with blasphemy and had condemned Him to death. The Jews, however, did not have the authority under Roman law to put a man to death, so they bound Him and took Him to Pontius Pilate, who was the Roman Governor over Jerusalem.

Pilate, in preparation for an audience with the accusers, had just sat down upon the judgment seat when his wife came to him. It was not a common practice for her to come to him while he was doing business and he was surprised to see her. "Why are you here?" he asked, "Is there something wrong?"

"Yes, my husband, I am sorry for the interruption but I had a dream last night. The gods warned me about this man, Jesus," she advised. "You must not have anything to do with Him! He is a fair man and has been wrongly accused."

"What are you trying to tell me?" Pilate questioned.

"Please, do nothing that will cause the gods to be angry! Do not condemn Him to death. I am afraid of what might happen if you do."

Pilot listened to his wife. He knew from past experiences that there was truth in her dreams. "Do not be so over-wrought," he consoled. "I will take your warning under advisement, but you must go now and let me do what is expected or me."

He waited for his wife to leave the room and then ordered that the prisoner and His accusers be brought before him. "What accusations do you have against this man?" he asked.

"He has broken our law."

"I am a Roman. I know nothing of your laws," he said and waved the accusers away. "You take Him and judge Him yourselves. You are asking me to bring judgment in a matter that has nothing to do with me or the Roman Government."

"We beg your humble pardon, we have found Him to be guilty, but, because of your law, we can not put Him to death."

"What guilt have you found in Him?" Pontius Pilot asked.

118

"Blasphemy! He claims that He is King of the Jews," they replied.

"Do you say that you are the King of the Jews?" Pilot asked of Jesus.

"Are you accusing me of this or did the others accuse me?" Jesus replied.

Pilot threw his hands up in total frustration and replied, "Am I a Jew? I don't know your beliefs or laws. It is your own nation and it is your Chief Priest that has delivered you to me. What have you done? Answer in your defense."

"I can only tell you that my kingdom is not of this world," Jesus replied.

"Then you are a King?"

"You have said that I am a King."

"I do not say that You are King," Pontius Pilot replied, and then turned to the accusers. "Has this man stolen anything? Has He murdered anyone? Does He kick jackals?"

"No, He has done none of those things."

"Then, why are you wasting my time? I find nothing that He has done is worthy of the punishment of death," Pontius Pilot replied.

He thought the Priests and Pharisees had very little grounds on which to condemn Jesus, and he was concerned about the warning that his wife had given to him earlier. He started to form a plan in his head...perhaps, if he gave them a graceful way out, they would drop the charges. He stood up, walked over to the group, and quietly spoke to the accusers, "You have a custom that I should release unto you a prisoner at the Passover. Would you like me to release this man you call 'King of the Jews'?"

The Jews huddled together and replied, "Please, let the people decide." They reasoned that if they could plant enough people in the crowd who would cry out to crucify Jesus then the people would not accuse them of the crucifixion.

"It will be so," replied Pontius Pilot, reasoning that if he brought out Barabbas, the most dreaded murderer he had in prison, the people would surely not want him released and Jesus would be set free. "Bring Barabbas here before me," he ordered.

"Thank you, Pontius Pilot," said the High Priest, "we are greatly appreciative of your fair and swift way of handling our situation. We will take our leave now."

After they got out of hearing range, he and the others plotted to pay the beggars and commoners to accuse Jesus when Pilot brought Him and Barabbas to stand before them. "Hurry, we have little time," he reminded them.

When Pilot took Barabbas and Jesus out on the balcony to stand before the people, he was shocked to see the multitude that had collected in the street. However, wanting to get the entire ordeal over with and get on with more important agendas, he looked down at them and said in a loud voice, "It is your custom on the day of the Passover feast that I release one prisoner. I stand before you with two prisoners, one is a gentle man called Jesus, and the other is the murderer named Barabbas. Of the two, which would you like for me to release?"

"Barabbas! Release Barabbas!" the multitude cried out.

"But why, what evil has Jesus done? Why do you insist that I crucify Him?" questioned Pontius Pilot.

"Let Him be crucified. He tried to make Himself King. By doing so, He speaks out against Caesar," they replied.

"I find no fault in this man," said Pilot. "Bring me a basin with water, so that I might wash my hands of this injustice. From this moment on, I am innocent of this man's blood. You crucify Him, for I will not." He reluctantly released Barabbas, the insurrectionist, robber and murderer. With a saddened heart he turned over Jesus, the man who taught only love, to His accusers who were determined to crucify Him.

The soldiers took Jesus to the common hall, blindfolded Him and tied His hands behind His back. They struck Him over and over again with a reed stick and, because He was blindfolded, He was unable to avoid the blows that landed full force. They beat Him until his eyes were swollen shut and His face a mass of bruises. They draped Him with a purple robe and forced a crown of thorns upon his head, scratching His brow severely and causing His blood to trickle down His face.

"Look at Him! See how He bleeds! He is a common man like you or I," scoffed a soldier. "He is a disgrace to the race," he said and then spat in His face. Because Jesus' hands were bound behind His back He could not wipe away the spittle and it remained dangling from His face.

"Here, take this whip and scourge Him, let us see where else he bleeds," taunted another. "I have tied a rock to the end of it so it will cut deep."

The soldier took the whip and began to whirl it with great speed above his head and then whipped it at Jesus, sinking it deep into His flesh and cutting to the bone. Again and again he whipped it at Jesus until the force of the lash began to injure the internal organs. He was near death when they finally placed the heavy rough-hewn cross upon His raw bleeding back to start the final journey to Golgotha.

* * *

Niccoli, totally unaware of what was happening, was extremely happy to have Master back in Jerusalem. She had already started arranging her week around the time she planned to spend with Him when suddenly she heard someone yelling, "They are taking Him to be crucified! They are going to crucifying Jesus!" The messenger ran down the street telling everyone that he met of the horrible event. "They are taking Him to the Place of the Skull at this very moment!" he cried.

Shocked beyond belief, Niccoli froze where she stood,

Why would they crucify her Lord? What had He ever done in His life to deserve the punishment of death? Surely the messenger was mistaken. The Roman government had no reason to condemn Him. Besides, God would never allow such a thing to happen. But, what if it were true? She had to see for herself and darted out the door and into the street. She had only taken a few steps when she saw Mary running towards her.

"Have you heard?" Mary gasped between breaths. "I cannot believe it is true! We must go see for ourselves!"

Niccoli nodded in response, barely taking enough time to acknowledge Mary. As they rounded the last corner before Golgotha, they could see the procession of people going to the hill, their silhouettes black against the morning sky. Above them on top of the hill stood a cross.

"No!" wailed Niccoli. "Please, don't let it be Jesus!" She looked helplessly at Mary who was staring straight ahead as though she was in shock. Niccoli took her hand and without another word they continued on, hoping against hope that it was all a mistake.

They pushed through a crowd of people huddled at the base of the hill and Niccoli recognized many who, only a few days prior, had laid palm leaves upon the ground for Jesus to trod over when He had entered Jerusalem. Now, in fear for their own lives, they were watching from afar.

Even though Niccoli had never witnessed a crucifixion, she had heard that the death was slow and agonizing for the prisoner. She was hesitant about going any further but she had to know if Jesus was one of the three, so she cautiously moved forward and as she approached the top of the hill she could see a cross lying on the ground. The prisoner was standing beside it, cursing the Roman soldiers and screaming for help as he struggled with every ounce of strength he had to free himself from their grip. It took four soldiers to wrestle him to the ground and bind his arms and feet to the cross.

"How horrible!" she uttered to herself. Her eyes searched the area and they fell upon Mary, the mother of Jesus, standing to one side. She was quietly sobbing, and the disciple John was standing beside her trying to comfort her.

"Oh, it is true!" Niccoli cried. "But why?"

She started towards Mother Mary, but was stopped short when an agonizing cry of pain drowned out the sound of hammers pounding nails. Niccoli turned to see what was happening, but the Roman soldiers who were crowded together blocked her view. She pushed her way forward and the scene before her made her violently ill. There, lying on the ground was another cross with the body of Jesus stretched out on top of it and the Roman soldiers were actually pounding nails into the flesh of His hands and feet! The pain etched upon His face was more than Niccoli could bear and she rushed forward.

"Stop! How can you do such a thing?" she cried out as she fought to rescue her Master. "He has done no wrong!"

"Step aside!" yelled one of the Romans. He glared at Niccoli as he took the back of his arm and shoved her away with such force that she fell to the ground. "Do not interfere or you will find yourself hanging from another cross!"

Contempt filled her as she glared at the Roman. Oh, how she wished she were a man. She would pull her sword and challenge him on the spot. If only her father were here, he would put a stop to all of this.

"Niccoli, he means what he says," a voice said as a hand reached down to help her. Niccoli looked up to see Andrew standing beside her. "There is little we can do now," he affirmed.

"But it is Jesus!" Niccoli sobbed. "There is no justification for this."

"Yes, I know," he replied sadly.

Niccoli again heard the blows of the hammer echo across the valley and the sound resounded in her ears. "Why don't they stop?" she asked Andrew and buried her head in his shoulder to escape the reality of what was happening. "Stop! Stop!" she cried as she crumpled his robe around her mouth to muffle the sound of her cries.

She felt totally helpless and could not stop her body from trembling. The shock of what was happening was just too much for her to accept. No matter how hard she tried to stop trembling, she could not.

She watched as the Romans carried the cross, with its victim attached, to the designated hole that had been dug earlier. They struggled with the weight of it but finally got it upright and then, with a final thrust, pushed it over the edge and let it drop into the hole with a thunderous jolt.

The sound of Jesus' agonizing cry pierced the air as the weight of His body hung suspended from the two large nails that had been pounded into His hands. His flesh around the nails pulled away from His bones and beads of perspiration popped out on His brow as He felt the agonizing pain.

Niccoli covered her ears with her hands and wailed. She felt as though she could not endure another injustice to her Lord. Why had they pounded nails into His hands? Why didn't they bind His hands with the leather straps, as they had bound the other two?

Niccoli saw the priests strutting in their glorious robes at the foot of the cross. "If you are the King of Israel, save yourself," they jeered. "Come down off the cross and we will believe in you." Laughingly, they pointed to the sign nailed to the cross over Jesus' head that said: THIS IS JESUS, KING OF THE JEWS. "Some King you are! Just look at you!" they mocked.

Their full intent was to embarrass Him in front of His followers. By crucifying Him like a common criminal they hoped that His followers would no longer believe in Him and would scatter. The threat to their leadership would then be crushed.

Niccoli felt so helpless. She watched as Jesus endured His pain without a word. She wanted to take Him into her arms and console Him. If only she could convince Him to perform one of His miracles and free Himself because she knew that if He had the power to heal her, He also had the power to save Himself and prevent His own suffering. So, why didn't He? Why was He putting Himself through such pain when one word would prevent it all? She simply did not understand why all of this was happening.

She turned to look at Mary, the mother of Jesus, and could see her son's pain reflected in her face as she watched Him suffer. When Jesus turned His head towards His mother Niccoli heard Him say, **"Woman, behold thy son,"** and then turning His gaze to John He said, **"Behold thy mother."**

"Yes, Master. It will always be so!" John replied.

Niccoli felt as though she was eavesdropping when she heard Jesus make the final arrangements to care for His mother. She watched as John put his arm around Mary in response to Jesus' request, and saw Mary bury her head in his shoulder and wail uncontrollably.

"Mary," John said gently; trying to console her in the best way that he knew, "there is too much pain here for you to stay. There is nothing that you can do to prevent this horrible thing from happening, let me take you to my home. It is harder on Jesus to know that you are watching His agony and pain, and it is also much too hard on you. I am sure He wants to protect you from all of this as much as possible, and does not want you to stay and watch Him slowly die."

Mary objected at first and then reluctantly allowed John to guide her through the gathering of people. She stopped, turned back toward Jesus, took one last look at her son and whispered a final goodbye. Jesus returned her gaze and then closed His eyes and nodded to her, letting her know that she

was doing the right thing in going with John. Mary gasped and collapsed at John's feet.

Suddenly, even though it was the sixth hour, the sky grew very dark, and the crowd grew restless about Niccoli as they whispered nervously among themselves. They could not explain what was happening. Some turned and ran, afraid of what might happen to them, while others hovered a distance away from the cross.

Niccoli sat at the foot of the cross for three hours. Jesus had become very quiet and His head hung down in a lifeless state. Then, with every ounce of strength left in Him, she watched as He lifted His head and cried out. **"My God, My God, why hast thou forsaken Me?"**

Niccoli remembered the despair that she had felt that night in the darkened alley and realized that Jesus was at this moment having those same feelings. She wanted so desperately for an end to all of the pain He was suffering.

"Father, into thy hands I commend my spirit," he whispered in an almost inaudible voice. There was one last breath and He fell totally limp.

Suddenly, the earth began to quake! Rocks broke in half as they rolled over each other, and Niccoli did not know whether to run or stay. The ground was shaking so much that she could not stand, and was terrified that it would open up and swallow her alive. Then, just as quickly as it had started, everything returned to normal. The quakes stopped and the darkness gave way to the sun as it again appeared in the sky.

"Truly Jesus was the Son of God!" a soldier cried and fell prostrate on the ground at the foot of the cross. "Forgive me! Oh, please, forgive me."

God must have loved His son very much to cause such turmoil! How else could one explain what had just happened?

CHAPTER 10

Judas watched as the four soldiers struggled to stand the cross upright, but the weight of Jesus made it very heavy and caused it to precariously sway back and forth. At one point Judas thought it would surely fall forward and crush Jesus beneath its weight...but then, perhaps falling on Him would be more merciful than the inevitable suffering that was in store for Him.

Everything had totally gotten out of control and Judas realized that he had played a major part in it. He had never expected Pilate to crucify Jesus. How could he have foreseen what was going to happen? Jesus was no criminal and He had broken no laws.

"Judas," Mary's voice broke his concentration, "isn't it horrible? I can not believe this is happening!"

"Nor can I, and I am going to do something about it!" Judas declared with determination. "They must listen to me!"

"Who must listen to you?" Mary questioned.

Judas ignored her. He was too engrossed in trying to figure a way to stop this horrible miscarriage of justice. A plan was starting to take form in his mind. Yes, he would take the thirty pieces of silver back to the priests and explain to them that they surely had misunderstood their agreement. If only he would be able to get there in time he could stop the crucifixion.

He pushed his way through the multitude, and raced through the streets of Jerusalem. Upon arrival at the temple he forced his way into the inner court and stormed in before the high priest. "You can't do it. You can't crucify Jesus!" he shouted. "You have made a terrible mistake. He has broken no criminal laws to justify the punishment of death. Send out an order now to Pilate and ask for the crucifixion to be stopped."

The priests, startled by the sudden interruption and the fact that someone would dare to disturb their quiet, stared at the intruder with disbelief. "What is the meaning of this?" demanded one. "Didn't we pay you enough? We deemed that He was not worthy of more."

"You were only to discredit him, not crucify him," replied Judas.

"Oh, you think so, do you? Well, now it is none of your concern. You turned him over to us and we paid you your thirty pieces of silver. Our business with you is finished! Do not disturb us any longer!" the high priest ordered.

"I will gladly return your money, just stop the execution!" Judas pleaded.

"I repeat! Your business with us is finished!" the high priest affirmed loudly, his voice was cold and unsympathetic. "I am no longer asking you to leave, I am now demanding that you leave!"

"You tricked me! It was never my intention to kill Jesus!" Judas yelled and threw the coins on the floor. "I no longer want your silver! You have made it blood money!"

The coins clattered as they hit upon the marble and scattered in every direction. One came to rest against the sandal of the high priest. He looked at it and paused before he stooped down to pick it up; when he straightened himself he held the coin up for Judas to see. "Make no mistake," he said in a clear distinct tone, "you were the one who deceived, not us. You were the one who betrayed your so-called Master, and accepted this coin as payment for leading us to Jesus. It was you who was the betrayer; we will do nothing to stop His execution!" he growled. "Now, leave us immediately!"

Judas stood rooted in disbelief. How could this be happening?

"Guards, escort this man from the temple!" the high priest ordered loudly.

"You can't kill Jesus!" screamed Judas. "You just can't, you cannot kill him!" he screamed repeatedly as he ran from one priest to another. The guards rushed him and punched him in the belly, causing him to fall forward in agony. They grabbed him under the arms and lifted him up until only the tip of his toes touched the floor. Laughing at his pain they hurriedly carried him down the corridor, but Judas regained his composure in enough time to yell back at the priests, "You will be sorry for this!"

He kicked at the guards in a vain attempt to free himself, but soon, when he realized that his efforts were fruitless, his screams subsided into murmuring and he went limp in their arms.

The guards looked at each other and rolled their eyes, neither could understand what he was saying and were totally convinced that he had gone mad. When they reached the outer courtyard they threw him in a heap on the ground, laughed uproariously then disappeared.

There were many people standing nearby but they kept their distance, hesitant to help anyone who had just been thrown out of the temple.

"Are you alright?" questioned the braver of the bystanders. "What did you do to deserve such reprisal?" He was very curious about what he had seen and could tell that the man on the ground appeared like a mad man only because he was seriously upset.

Judas made no response. He was not even aware of the

fact that someone had spoken to him. "Jesus, forgive me!" he mumbled over and over again. "I knew not what they were going to do. Forgive me. Oh, **please** forgive me!"

The stranger leaned forward in an effort to hear what Judas was saying. Unable to understand the words he determined that Judas was delirious and shook him by his shoulders. Again he asked, "Are you alright?"

Judas looked up, his eyes were full of fright and lifted his hands to shield his head and face.

"I am not going to hurt you," responded the stranger.

Judas did not answer him and then, as if struck by a lightening bolt, he jumped up, let out a whimper and ran out of the courtyard into the street screaming, "Please, please, forgive me!" Running as fast as he could, Judas disappeared; leaving behind people who were not the least bit interested in getting involved.

"Was that not one of the disciples of Jesus?" someone queried.

Most just shrugged their shoulders and continued with whatever they were doing before the interruption. "Who cares," responded one.

* * *

The priests did not want the bodies of the three crucified men to hang on the crosses over the most high Sabbath day of the year, so they went to Pilate and asked that the legs of the men be broken to hasten their deaths. Pilate granted the request, complaining that the Jews were driving him crazy with their stupid laws and superstitions. He sent the order out to the soldiers and they broke the legs of the first two, but when they approached Jesus they realized that He was already dead and they passed Him by. However, one of the soldiers, angry and frustrated because of his forced participation in the crucifixion drew his sword and thrust it into Jesus' side.

Immediately blood and water gushed from the wound and onto the soldier. "Get it off me!" he screamed as he grabbed for the nearest thing to wipe the blood from his arm.

"Drop that robe!" yelled another as he grabbed it from the hysterical soldier. "Don't you dare stain this robe with blood! It is the robe of Jesus and I claim it now. Some Christian will pay me a dear price to obtain possession of it."

"Who left you in charge of things?" yelled the third soldier as he grabbed for the robe. "I do not remember that Jesus gave His robe to any one of us. That being true, I have just as much right to it as any one of you. I lay claim to it!"

"I had it first," snapped the first soldier and jerked the robe from the grasp of the third.

"What is going on there?" the centurion yelled as he rushed forward, his full attention now directed on the quarreling soldiers. "Why do you argue over a pauper's robe?"

"It is not just a pauper's robe," explained the second soldier. "Many people followed and believed in Him. It will be worth much to one of them. It was my idea to sell the robe and I lay claim to it."

"If this robe is so valuable you will all cast lots for it," the angry centurion declared. He turned to the remaining soldiers and barked in a booming voice, "Listen up! Who would like to cast lots for the robe of this man called Jesus?"

All of the soldiers scrambled to get a chance at the robe. The thrill of gambling was always great fun, it was of little consequence to them if they wanted the robe or not. They threw the robe on the ground before them and huddled together, jeering and cursing at each other as they drew their lots.

Niccoli loathed the soldiers and the games that they played. How dare they demean her Savior like that? She wanted to grab the robe and hold it close to her bosom. She was still shaking from anger when she saw Joseph of Arimathea walk past her. She changed her focus and watched him discuss with his servants how to take the badly bruised and bleeding body of Jesus from the cross.

"We need to lift the cross out of the hole and then carefully lay it down on the ground," contemplated Joseph. "It will not be an easy task with no more men than we have because it will be extremely heavy with His body hanging upon it, but we must get it into a position where we will be able to have the leverage to pull the nails out of His hands and feet. I know of no other way than to lay the cross flat upon the ground."

The servants looked at him and shook their heads. "It is going to be extremely top heavy. How will we be able to keep it from falling?" asked the elder one.

"First, we must dig out the dirt that is packed around the base of the cross so that we can lift it from the ground and lay it down," replied Joseph. "Michael, you will put your back against the cross to stabilize it until the top of the cross is lowered far enough so that I can grasp it. Be aware Michael, that you will have the full weight of the cross and Jesus' body until I am able to help you. Are you up to it?"

"I certainly hope so," replied Michael with an uncertain shake of his head.

After the dirt was dug out, and the cross was to the point of toppling, they positioned themselves in their assigned places and Michael put his back against the backside of it. On the count of three the servants strained against the weight and pushed the cross back until it slowly began to fall. Joseph watched and waited until the upper portion was low enough for him to help with its weight and guide it to ground with Jesus' body still intact. With their mission accomplished the men breathed a sigh of relief and fell to the ground in total exhaustion.

"Who will remove the nails?" asked the elder.

There was a long silence before Joseph reluctantly replied, "I will." The nails were driven so far into the wood that it was difficult for Joseph to loosen them. Nausea flooded over him and his brow glistened with perspiration as he tapped the nail from side to side with his mallet until it loosened enough to enable him to remove it. He repeated the procedure until all three nails were finally removed. He stared at the nails on the ground before him and then picked them up and flung them as far as he could before slumping to the ground, angry at what had been done to his Master.

Niccoli wailed as she came forward and knelt down beside Jesus. She pulled His body onto her lap and cradled His head close to her bosom as she rocked back and forth. "Why?" she cried out. "Why did they do this?"

Joseph stood quietly and allowed time for Niccoli to grieve, but when she showed no signs of relinquishing Jesus he said softly, "Niccoli, it is time for us to take Him to the tomb." But Niccoli shook her head; she could not bear to give Him up.

"I understand," Joseph sympathized, "but it must be." He loosened her grip, pulled her away from the body and sat her on the ground nearby. He wrapped Jesus in a blanket and, with the help of his servants, picked Him up and started for the tomb.

Niccoli fell into place with the procession. She looked around for her friend Mary and saw her a short distance away. She walked over to her and together they wailed the cry of death as they made their way to the nearby tomb that Joseph had originally prepared for himself.

Nicodemus was waiting at the tomb with the linen clothes to soak in the mixture of aloes and myrrh that he had prepared. When he saw Niccoli and Mary he motioned for them to come to his side. "Would you please help us?" he asked. "Soak the clothes in this mixture and then hand them to either me or Joseph."

The women did as he said and soon they were binding Jesus from head to foot. When they had finished, the men carried Him inside the tomb and laid Him out on the cold rock slab that jetted out from the side of the cavern. Joseph placed a fresh linen napkin over His face and lingered, along with Nicademus, for a few minutes. Neither wanted to say that final farewell to the one they had held holy.

The Roman guards waited until the two men emerged from the tomb then rolled the huge stone in front of the entrance and watched as it fell to rest in the hole that had been dug to keep the huge stone in place and seal the tomb. The guards took their places as the high priests had ordered them to do; making sure that none of Jesus' followers would steal the body and claim that He had risen from the dead as He had predicted. Stationing the guards was a precaution to keep that from happening.

The day had been a horrible nightmare and Niccoli was exhausted. Without another word she turned away and started for home. Mary walked beside her in silence until they were in sight of Niccoli's home. "Niccoli, I am frightened!" she finally blurted out. She had been afraid to speak out earlier, for fear someone would be listening. "What if they come after us and the others?"

"I know," responded Niccoli, "I also have been thinking about that. Perhaps we should keep a low profile until things calm down. The ones I fear for the most are the disciples. I think that they are in great danger."

"At this point I don't think any of us are safe," Mary cautioned.

"Do you wish to stay with me for awhile?" asked Niccoli.

"Thank you, but no. I have to keep up with my students. I will be careful. I just need to be more aware of what is happening around me. Shalom, Niccoli."

"Shalom," replied Niccoli. She watched Mary until she turned the corner. Yes, there was no doubt, they must watch out for each other. When she entered her home it seemed just as cold and empty as her heart felt at that moment. What a horrible ending to the Passover! It would never again be the joyous celebration that it had been in the past. Now it would always remind her of a roughly hewn cross and a man hanging in unbearable pain.

The next morning Sarah and Niccoli walked slowly on their way to Jesus' tomb to burn the incense. It was so hard to accept the fact that He was gone and, even though the burning of incense was important, Niccoli thought the true reason that they were there was because they felt closer to Him by just being next to His body.

Niccoli took her vigil on a nice flat rock beside the path which was not too close to the tomb but close enough for her incense to be effective. The rock was large enough to be able to spread out her blanket and comfortably sit upon it while having her incense bowl in front of her. After she lit her incense she sat quietly thinking about all of the dreams and promises for the future that had died along with Jesus.

Sarah was the first to break the silence. "Niccoli, did you hear about Judas?"

"No, I haven't seen him since the crucifixion," she replied.

"Nor will you, he hung himself!" Sarah replied, visibly emotional and on the verge of tears.

"What!" exclaimed Niccoli? She studied Sarah's face and could not tell if her friend was angered or saddened by the news. "Where did you hear that? Why would he have done such a thing?"

"Well, I understand it was for thirty pieces of silver," answered Sarah.

Confused, Niccoli asked, "What are you trying to say?"

"Simple, he betrayed Jesus for thirty pieces of silver," Sarah revealed angrily. "He led the soldiers to Jesus and kissed Him upon the cheek to identify Him."

"You can't mean that," Niccoli stated, shocked to think that Judas could do such a thing, but the look on Sarah's face confirmed that she was quite serious. "I didn't know," Niccoli said softly. "For him to turn over Jesus is so hard to believe! But then again, that may explain all the money I saw him counting when I stopped by their abode. I thought it strange that there was so much, and he was very nervous about me seeing it. I am so shocked to hear all of this because he was always so kind to me."

"You were always giving him money for his pouch," scoffed Sarah, "no wonder he was kind to you."

"It is true I shared with them the money I received from dancing before the multitudes while they were waiting for Jesus," mused Niccoli, "and I do remember that sometimes he was rather rude to the people, but he was never harsh with anyone. It is so hard to believe he was so cruel to Jesus."

"Well, it must have been true or he would not have hung himself. He probably was sorry and could not face what he had done," Sarah said with finality.

"We must pray for his soul," Niccoli replied.

The two fell silent, each lost in their own thoughts, as they pondered over all the events of the last two days. Soon the shadows grew long and the sun started to set. "Sarah, we must start for home, Jacob will be coming after us if we are still here after the sun goes down," Niccoli declared.

"Yes, I know, Jacob is too protective sometimes but in the end I am glad he is that way. My wish for you is that you will find someone who is as kind and gentle as he. I rather like Andrew; he has some very good qualities and is a follower of Jesus. That is a very big plus and I know that he is infatuated with you."

"Yes, he is a very good friend, but I am fine just the way things are now," laughed Niccoli as she fell into step with Sarah. "My life is quite comfortable and I feel no need for a serious relationship. For now, my friendship with Andrew is fulfilling enough and I need nothing else."

Long after Niccoli had slipped into bed that night, she

found that sleep was very difficult and was awake most of the night. Every time she closed her eyes she would see Jesus stretched out upon the cross and heard the sound of the hammer as it pounded the nails into her Master's flesh. She put her hands over her ears and tried to stop His agonizing cries as they echoed in her memory. When she finally fell asleep it was almost morning and it seemed that she had only slept for a few minutes before she was awakened by what seemed to her to be loud pounding on her front door. She struggled to open her eyes, shook her head in an effort to awaken and realized someone was knocking on the front door.

"Niccoli, are you awake?" called out Sarah. She was on her way to the tomb again and had stopped by for Niccoli as they had planned.

Niccoli strained to get herself out of bed and answer the door. "Yes, Sarah, come in," she said drowsily as she opened the door. "I had a terrible night and did not fall to sleep until early this morning. I am sorry I overslept, I will be ready to go momentarily," apologized Niccoli.

"That is alright, I understand perfectly. I also had a lot of trouble sleeping last night," replied Sarah. "All I could think of was the horror of the crucifixion."

"I know. All I could hear was the hammering of the nails and the cries of Jesus."

Niccoli dressed quickly and was soon ready to go. She gave Sarah a weak smile as she picked up her incense, blanket and bowl that she had left in a neat stack near the front door. "I think," she said as she opened the door, "I am ready for another sorrowful day."

The morning was a typical cool spring morning in Jerusalem and the dew was still on the ground as they walked in silence down the dirt street. It was Sarah that was the first to break the silence. "Niccoli," she spoke softly, "do you realize that today is the third day. How long do you think the guards will watch the tomb?"

Niccoli shrugged her shoulders and kicked at a pebble with the toe of her sandal. She caught up with it and gave it another kick before she said anything. "They are afraid someone will steal the body," she responded. "I would guess that they will stand guard for days because they are so paranoid. I wish they would leave! They treat us as though we were common criminals."

Mary was also on her way to the tomb. As planned she had purchased more incense and was but a short distance in front of Niccoli and Sarah. Suddenly she saw a glow through the trees. She had never before seen such a thing and was hesitant about continuing and, although she felt drawn to the strangeness of the light, proceeded around the bend in the road with caution until she was in full view of the light. Amazed at the brilliance of it, she shielded her eyes and realized that it was enveloping Jesus' tomb. As she tried to understand what was happening, she saw an angel descend from the heavens and stop at the huge stone that had been rolled in front of the tomb's opening. She watched the angel effortlessly roll the stone and could feel the ground tremor as the rock rolled off to one side. She looked for the guards and saw them lying lifeless on the ground nearby and wondered if perhaps they were dead.

"Do not be afraid nor saddened," The angel consoled as he smiled at her. With a flutter of his wings he flew to the top of the stone and sat down before continuing. "I know that you have come to be close to Jesus, but He is not here! He has risen from the dead as He said He would. Did you not watch as I rolled the stone away and know that He did not exit. Come, see for yourself; the tomb is empty."

Mary cautiously moved forward and peered into the tomb. The linen cloths that had bound His body were lying there and the napkin that had been placed over His head was folded and put in a separate place. She remembered that He had raised Lazarus from the dead. Did He do the same for himself? If so, where was He?

When Niccoli and Sarah arrived Mary urged them to also look inside the tomb. Stunned, they turned to the angel for further explanation of what was happening.

"Tell His disciples that He has risen from the dead and He will meet them in Galilee. Now, go quickly!" the angel instructed them. Instantly he was gone, the light subsided and the garden was once again totally silent.

The women looked at each other and were filled with conflicting emotions. They knew that they must do as the angel had told them but they were afraid as well as joyful. Without a word, they turned and started running to find the disciples. They had not gotten far when Niccoli stopped abruptly in the middle of the road and grabbed Sarah's arm. "Sarah, look!" she cried breathlessly, "Do you see what I see?"

"Yes, it is another angel," was the reply.

"No, it is the Lord!" exclaimed Mary as she broke into a run.

"Rejoice!" said Jesus as He greeted them. **"Do not be afraid. Tell My disciples to meet Me in Galilee. There they will be able to see Me."**

The women fell at His feet and worshiped Him.

"Oh, Master, it is really you!" sobbed Mary. She started to throw her arms around His neck but Jesus stopped her.

"You can not touch my body. I have not yet gone to My Father," he explained. **"Now, go and do as I have asked of you. I promise, I will be with you again."**

Yes, Master," the women responded in unison and reluctantly turned away. Soon, however, they were running as fast as they could to share the good news with the disciples. Their Jesus was alive!

* * *

When the guards regained consciousness they went to the high priest and told him what had happened. The high priest, disturbed that the disappearance of Jesus might cause a rebellion, assembled together the elders and other priests to consult with them and determine what to do about the empty tomb. When they finally came to a decision, they called the soldiers before them.

"I have a large sum of money for each of you," the high priest told them. "In return you are to tell the people that Jesus' disciples came in the night and stole His body. This order is to be sealed with secrecy. Do you understand? You must never tell anyone what really happened today!"

"What happens if the governor should hear of this conspiracy?" asked one of the soldiers.

"How could he say otherwise? There is only a conspiracy if one of you say that there is," replied an elder.

"Then it will be so," the soldier agreed.

CHAPTER 11

The Christian people scattered, afraid to admit they had followed Jesus for fear that they also would be persecuted. Even the chosen twelve were in hiding, but soon after Jesus appeared to them they started teaching again, witnessing that He had risen from the dead and was indeed a living Savior.

Andrew, knowing that there would be strength in numbers, became instrumental in banding the Christian people together. He had little time for anything else and worked hard to make sure that they did not openly anger the Jewish priests.

One major difference between the Christians and the Jews was that the Christian movement allowed all people to participate in the worship service. They allowed women to not only worship in the same room with the men, but to also teach and encourage other people to meet with them. Because the Jewish tradition was so deeply imbedded in the community, any indication that a woman was speaking out in public brought the wrath of the Jews down upon all Christian women. Women, in the Jewish opinion, were to only speak through their husbands and hold to his beliefs. They were never to express their own feelings.

Niccoli, one of the most outspoken, was especially at risk.

She offered her home as a meeting place for the Christian community and worked side by side with Andrew to make the church a success. She was proud of how he could organize people and guide them with a firm but gentle hand. His organizational skills made the movement grow rapidly, and the Christians looked up to him and trusted him without question.

One autumn afternoon when Andrew entered Niccoli's home to prepare for the evening gathering, he was met by Niccoli's excited greeting, "Andrew, look who is here!" she exclaimed as she hurried towards him.

"John!" Andrew called out. "It has been so long since we have seen you!" He hurried to embrace his friend, one of the chosen twelve, and held him at arms length as he continued, "It is really you! My brother, it is so good to see you! Come, sit with me for a while. When did you arrive?"

"Only a short time ago," John answered. "I have been hearing good things about you. From the sounds of it you have things under control here."

"I only wish," Andrew laughed, then grew somber. "I pray every day that the Jewish priests and elders will be more accepting of us, and that we will soon be able to come out into the open with our beliefs. It would be wonderful to share the love of Jesus with everyone without being fearful. Tell me, how are things going in other cities?"

"About the same as here. I am sad to report that people are afraid," responded John. "As you well know, they have just cause to feel the way they do. I recently received news from Rome that the Christians are in very real danger. Nero seems to fear an uprising and has been killing all Christians that he can find. That is one of the reasons I would like to speak to the people who will be here tonight. With your permission, I need to reassure them that Jesus is risen and is very much alive."

"Of course you have my permission, they would be disappointed if you did not speak to them. Besides, they get tired of hearing me all the time!" chuckled Andrew.

"I always enjoy your humor, we certainly need that today," John gave his friend a pat on the shoulder. "Now, I have something I want to discuss with the two of you."

"We are listening," replied Andrew.

John was always happy to be with dedicated people who loved his Lord but Andrew and Niccoli were two of his favorites. "I have a request to make," he continued. "And I hope that you will say yes. Since you have done such a wonderful job in teaching and organizing the people here in Jerusalem, I would like for you to go to other towns and help them get organized. They are in dire need of leadership and the two of you would be of great help to them. Before you answer, I want to warn you that if you agree to this it will, undoubtedly, put you at even greater risk. Remember James, Jesus' brother, was mobbed and killed here in Jerusalem, and James, my brother, was killed by Herod for speaking his beliefs."

"John, I can not speak for Niccoli, but I am at the Lord's disposal," replied Andrew. "If you think that this is what I should be doing to help make His kingdom become recognized, then I will do wherever you feel is needed."

"There is no question, I will also go," assured Niccoli.

"Good!" John confirmed. "We will discuss more details later, perhaps after the meeting or early in the morning."

Andrew and Niccoli spread the word that John was going to speak in the evening and most everyone was able to attend. John's affect on the Christians was as though he had taken the words of Jesus and made them into a lightning bolt that struck the Christian community, charging them with the energy needed to continue God's work.

After John left, Niccoli and Andrew discussed the possibility of preaching in other villages. They both agreed that they were called to help others and they needed to take John's request very seriously, but there was one major problem that they had to address; who would lead the church in their absence. After they had thoroughly discussed the matter, they confirmed three names.

Now, the only decision they had to make was where they needed to go that would be of the most help to the Christian community. They mulled over several possibilities and eventually determined that they should make their way along the mountain range to the Sea of Galilee, stopping at Samaria, Nazareth, Cana and, possibly, Capernaum.

Even though the Christians of the smaller churches warmly welcomed Niccoli and Andrew, they could still feel the hostility among the Jewish people of the community. However, they did not let that deter them from doing what they were sent to accomplish, and they immediately started their ministry by encouraging the people to keep their faith and to help them organize their groups.

Niccoli cherished the moments that she spent with them. She shared the lessons of love and forgiveness that Jesus had taught her, and described the many miracles that she had witnessed as she followed Him throughout the countryside. The people listened intently, hungry for any first hand accounts of His teachings. They especially loved to hear her recount the miracle of her own healing and how she had given up her Roman gods for the God of Jesus.

The most touching moment of all was when she told them of her experience at the crucifixion. She would always be overcome with emotion whenever she told the story. She could not fathom the agony that Jesus had felt; not only for the torture He had endured, but also for the hurt He must have felt by the betrayal of His own disciple, Judas, who had turned Him over to the High Priest for thirty pieces of silver. His heart must have been broken, but despite His agony and hurt He had asked for His Father to forgive all who had done an injustice to Him. That included Judas. If she had not witnessed this love, she would not have believed that such love was possible.

One evening, after their meeting with the Christians, she and Andrew were walking in the direction of the home where they were staying when suddenly they saw several men and women immerge from an alley and block the roadway ahead of them. "She Devil! Blasphemer!" they yelled at Niccoli.

Niccoli was shocked. "Andrew, are these people angry at me?" she questioned. "I have done nothing to them? I do not even know them."

"Do not listen to them, Niccoli," whispered Andrew as he took her arm and turned away to avoid them. He quickened their pace but they had barely turned when a rock hit Niccoli in the middle of her back. She fell to her knees screaming in pain.

"Leave this village," someone yelled. "We do not want your kind here!"

Another rock was hurled through the air and fell at Andrew's feet. Trying to protect Niccoli the best that he could, he ignored their aggressors and hurriedly helped Niccoli to her feet. Together they ran looking for shelter with the people in close pursuit behind them, throwing rocks and anything else that they could get their hands upon at the woman who spoke out for her beliefs.

"Andrew, what are we going to do?" Niccoli gasped between breaths. "We can not lead them to our friends' home."

"Look! There is a stable...run for it!" yelled Andrew and pulled Niccoli in front of him to protect her, but it was too late, another rock had already found its mark and hit her on the back of her leg.

"Stop," she cried out as she stumbled forward. "Please God, make them stop!"

Another few feet and they were inside the stable. Andrew slammed and bolted the door only seconds before the crowd caught up with them. They fell breathless upon the hay that was stacked in a corner and listened to the crowd jeer and bang upon the door for what seemed like hours. Finally the jeering stopped and the crowd quieted. Andrew rose and looked out of the window; to his relief the Jews were beginning to disperse, each feeling smug that they had proven their point.

"They are starting to leave," he told Niccoli.

"Thank God!" she sighed.

"We will stay here for the night. I don't think they will bother us anymore, but neither do I want to take any chances," Andrew stated and then turned his attention to Niccoli's wounds. "Let me see where you were hit. Do you feel as though any bones were broken?"

"I don't think so," she sobbed, "but I hurt so badly!"

"You took some nasty hits! Your back is bleeding. I'll look for some water, or even better maybe some wine. Perhaps the caretaker has some hidden somewhere."

Andrew searched the stable and soon he had a wine flask in his hand. "See I told you there would be wine hidden here," he said. "Brace yourself, this might sting a little," he warned and proceeded to pour it on Niccoli's wounds. When he had finished cleaning the wounds he smiled and said, "Get some sleep now. I will keep watch."

Niccoli relaxed and stretched out on the hay. She was so extremely grateful for Andrew's gentleness and caring. Having complete faith in his ability to watch over her she smiled a thank you before drifting off to sleep.

Andrew was aware of every sound outside the stable, and when he was confident that the accusers had disbursed he stretched out on the hay beside Niccoli. Propping himself on his elbow he watched her sleep and noticed how her long eyelashes lay curled on her cheek. His body ached for her and he wished that she had the same feelings for him but, sadly, she did not. He knew that to her he was only a good friend and fellow worshiper of Jesus. If only he could find a way to change her mind.

Night gave way to morning and there were no more attacks on Niccoli for the remainder of their visit in Cana. Two days before their scheduled day to continue on to the next city the horrible news came to them that Bartholomew, another disciple of Jesus, had been skinned alive! The news stabbed Niccoli's heart. She remembered how the stones had made her body ache and could not imagine the pain of being skinned alive. "Oh God, embrace Bartholomew, your child. He has experienced a ghastly death!" Niccoli prayed.

Andrew announced Bartholomew's death at the service that evening. There was a deaden silence as mothers clutched their children close to them and wives hung onto their husbands arms. All had tears in their eyes and fear was written across each face as they sat stunned in their seats. They were well aware that Bartholomew had been killed for speaking out about the God of love that they also loved and believed in. His death brought to their attention the full realization that they were also in grave danger. How could people reject a God who had given so much for them?

To make matters worse in Rome, Nero married his adulterous mistress, Poppaea, a Jewish woman who hated the Christians and exerted her influence over Nero. It became more and more impossible for the Christians to profess their beliefs. Tales of horror were coming out of Rome testifying to events that had taken place in which Nero killed and tortured many. He seemed to find great delight in their persecution, and it was no longer a matter of killing leaders of the Christian faith, but now entire families were being executed.

It became necessary to instruct the Christian women that they must remain silent in public for their own protection. It was Nero's belief that they had great influence over their husbands and Poppaea, because of her Jewish roots, believed that women should not have a voice in the church.

Because of the atrocities that were inflicted by Nero, the Roman Christians were forced to develop their own secret intricate underground system to protect themselves and their families from the ultimate threat. To identify one another, one person would draw a simple outline of the upper half of a fish and the other would finish the bottom outline. This same drawing was also used to gain admittance at meeting places.

Niccoli's heart went out to the Roman Christians and for some time she had been contemplating the possibility of returning to Rome. She thought that was the best way she could help her fellow Christians. There was also another reason for going back; to be near her mother who was in ill health. Being an only child Niccoli felt it was her duty to return to her mother's side and help in any way possible. When she heard the news about the Roman Christians she decided it was now time to return.

When she told Andrew of her decision to return to Rome he immediately set up a barrage of reasons explaining why she should not go. "Niccoli," he argued, "how could you possibly be thinking that you alone can make a difference? You are only one person! To go back to Rome would mean certain death!" His voice was loud and almost to the point of commanding because he was so upset with her reasoning.

"Well," she huffed, "you do not need to yell at me!"

"Niccoli, I am sorry, I do not intend to yell at you but listen to yourself. Do you honestly think that you could do more good in Rome than here?"

"Yes."

"Then you are foolish!" he said as he threw up his hands in despair.

"Oh, now I am foolish! Quit condemning me! You have no right."

"I have no right?" Andrew responded angrily. "Did I hear you correctly? I have no right? Am I not your friend? How can you say that to me? Niccoli, why don't you listen to me? I am only thinking of your safety."

"I am sorry, but it is my life! If Jesus wants me in Rome, then that is where I am going." She stomped her foot and turned her back on him. She was trying not to get upset with him because she knew how he felt about her, but she was really angry at his reaction.

She crossed her arms in stubborn rebellion, but slowly the guilt of their argument and her curt replies to him started to gnaw at her and she turned to face him. "Andrew," she said compassionately, "I am sorry that this upsets you. I truly do not wish to argue with you."

"Niccoli, please listen to me," he pleaded. "If you return to Rome you are not only putting yourself in danger but also your father and mother. Do you think the Roman government would embrace your father if they knew that he was harboring a Christian?"

"No, I know that they would not. I have thought about it a lot and it is one of the reasons that I have hesitated about going back sooner. I realize my presence may put them in danger. But Andrew, there is something you are forgetting. My mother is in ill health. Father says there is nothing else that the doctors can do for her and I need to be there by her side. I am their only child and there is no other to take my place. I need to return to Rome for her sake as well as for the Roman Christians. I love my mother and cannot bear to think that if I remain here I might never see her again. So, Andrew, you see there are two good reasons that I must to return to Rome."

"You are one persistent woman," responded Andrew knowing that he had lost the battle. But what could he do? He could only insist that he accompany her. "Then I am going with you," he declared solemnly.

"Now, it is my turn to tell you no. Father may be able to protect me in some way but you would probably have to be on your own. Besides, who will take over here?"

"There is more than one who would be quite capable of leading the people here. So, no room for discussion...I am going!" he responded firmly.

"If you insist," Niccoli responded. "I must confess that I will be glad to have you near. We have made a good team thus far and it would be a shame for anything or anyone to come between us. The thought of not working with you any longer has made me realize that I have come to depend upon you more than I had ever wanted to admit."

"Glad to hear you admit that," laughed Andrew as he threw his arms around her.

"Strictly the Lord's business," responded Niccoli with a smile.

Together they made plans for the journey that she had made years before when she sought out Mary's dance studio. This time, however, the excitement she had previously felt was missing, and in its place was the grim realization that they were most likely traveling to their deaths; the only question was when and how it might come about.

CHAPTER 12

Although Cornelius was extremely happy to have his daughter home again, he was very upset about her Christian activities. After all, he was a man of status in the Roman government and could not afford to get involved in such a controversial issue. It could very well mean that he would be, as the very least of punishments, stripped of his position. Besides, it was common knowledge that the Roman gods were the ultimate gods. They were strong and virile, far beyond anything that was capable of man. Lightning flashed from their fingertips and the heavens rumbled when they were angry. How could anyone defy that? Especially when she was the daughter of a Roman diplomat.

In Cornelius's mind, this man called Jesus had to have been some kind of a fanatic. He had allowed Himself to be hung on a cross like a common criminal. How could Niccoli follow so blindly someone who would not even stand up for Himself? His daughter's loyalty to such a God, or should he say common person, was far beyond his understanding.

Be that as it may, the fact remained that he loved her despite their differences and would protect her at all costs. He wanted no knowledge of her activities and reasoned that what he did not know could not be used against her, or him for that matter. Their safety was foremost in his mind and he would always act accordingly.

However, now he had to clear his mind of Niccoli's foolishness and return his thoughts to his yearly feast to which he had invited the Senate and other distinguished Diplomats. He had also invited a particular Centurion with whom he was impressed and who was in good standing with the Parliament. He recognized potential when he saw it and secretly hoped that Niccoli might take an interest in the Centurion and forget this Christian nonsense.

"Father," Niccoli said softly, "am I interrupting?"

"Niccoli, my child...nothing can ever be so important that you would be interruptive. As a matter of fact, I was just thinking of you. Please come in. Now I will not have to send for you."

"There is something you wish of me?" Niccoli asked.

"Yes, I wish for you to be at my side for my yearly feast."

"Oh, Father, you know I do not care for those types of events. I can only think of what they are allowing to happen to the Christians here in Rome. I cannot be polite to your Senate friends. So, I am sorry, but I must decline."

Cornelius rose and went to Niccoli. He put his arm around her and was quiet for a moment, trying to think of how he could convince her to do as he wanted. He was well aware of her contempt for what the Roman government was doing to the Christians and knew that it would be hard to persuade her to attend such a function, but he also knew how important it was to her to make him happy.

"Niccoli, pamper your poor father. You know how ill your mother is; there is no way that she will be able to attend. It saddens me that this will be the first year she will not be at my side. I will sorely miss her."

"Father, do not make me feel guilty," Niccoli pleaded, brushing his arm aside.

"It is not my intention to make you feel guilty. Nor is it

my will that your mother be critically ill." Cornelius looked at his daughter with large sad eyes.

"Very well, I will go in Mother's place, but you do not seem to understand how difficult it will be for me to do as you ask."

"Then it is decided!" Cornelius exclaimed and clapped his hands together in a gesture of final approval, his sad countenance now effaced with a glow of victory. "Now, why did you come to see me?"

"I wanted to hear what the doctors said about Mother. I so worry about her," Niccoli replied.

"As do I," Cornelius said sadly. "She has been a faithful wife and friend, but I fear the time is all too near for her to leave us. I wish it were different."

"There is nothing more the doctors can do?" sobbed Niccoli.

"No, nothing."

Niccoli bowed her head. 'Please, Lord, be with my mother in her final days,' she prayed silently and then looked at her father. "I will be there for you," she relented.

"Thank you. You have made a sad man very happy. I will send out for the loveliest dress in all of Rome. Wear your hair up with flowers woven through it. You have always looked so beautiful with your hair fixed in that manner."

"Yes, Father. Shalom."

"Niccoli!" Cornelius stammered, "Please do not use that word in my house."

"I am sorry," Niccoli apologized, "I will then say farewell."

Niccoli dressed early on the evening of the feast because she wanted time to stop by her mother's room. She knew Diana loved the gala event almost as much as Cornelius and she wanted her to feel included. She thought perhaps it would please her if she saw the dress that her father had chosen for her to wear. "Are you sleeping?" Niccoli whispered as she entered Diana's bedroom.

Diana stirred and opened her eyes. When she saw Niccoli she smiled and put forth her hand to welcome her daughter. "You are so beautiful!" she praised as she scanned Niccoli's attire. "I am glad you stopped to see me before the feast. It is times like this that I feel so left out. However, it gives me comfort to know that you are here to fill in for me."

"Yes, Mother, I am here for you."

"Your father picked out your gown? He always enjoyed doing that for me." Diana smiled with pride.

"Yes, Mother, he chose it."

"It needs a little something at the neck. Please, bring my jewel box to my side," Diana instructed. "I know just the necklace that will fit your neckline beautifully."

Niccoli rose and crossed the room to her mother's large ornate dresser. She opened the top drawer and took out a gold box that was hidden in the corner. Even though jewelry had little significance to Niccoli she knew how much it meant to her mother and smiled at her when she placed it in her hand.

"I have waited until the appropriate time to give you this," Diana explained. "It is the necklace that your father gave to me on the night of our engagement. After you, it has always been my most prized possession. I would feel honored for you to wear it tonight."

Diana lovingly picked up the ornate golden necklace laden with large emeralds, rubies and topazes and held it to her breast for a long moment. Tears came to her eyes as she remembered only the good times. Finally, with a feeble voice she said to her daughter, "Come, kneel beside me. I want you to wear it tonight." It was a strain for her to raise herself up so that she could place the precious necklace around her daughter's neck; but at last, after great effort, the clasp was fastened. She smiled, pleased at how it looked. She kissed Niccoli on the forehead and then col-lapsed back upon her pillow; weary from the energy it took to accomplish such a small feat.

"Are you alright, Mother?" Niccoli quickly jumped up to give her assistance.

"Yes, my daughter...and do not worry so. Erase that sad look on your face. I could not be happier than I am at this moment being with you. Now, go and see to your father's needs. The great orator gets very nervous about his dinner parties."

Niccoli smiled and tucked the covers around her mother's frail body. "Goodnight," she said as she kissed her on the forehead, "I will look in on you later." As she closed the door behind her she heard her mother call out softly, "Make your father proud."

Niccoli turned and hurried down the hall to the eloquently decorated banquet room. Cornelius had ordered bouquets of flowers to be placed on every pedestal available and one needed to walk but a few paces to find the finest wine and every delicacy imaginable. In an adjoining room he had displayed the feast with artistry unique to his ostentatious ways.

He was known throughout Rome for his yearly parties and they were considered the biggest and most grandiose event of the year. Only those who were considered to be Rome's elite were invited and the pretentious guests dressed in their finest, each trying to surpass the other. It was a known fact that to be added to Senator Cademus' guest list was a symbol that they had achieved society's highest honor and would now be accepted into the inner circle.

Niccoli hurried to her father's room to let him know that she was ready. She knew that he was probably pacing the floor by now and did not want to keep him waiting. Even though he had coached her earlier in the way that she should carry out her duties for the evening, she was sure that by now he had thought of something else that he needed to tell her. She understood how important this party was to him and how much he wanted to have everything go perfectly. She was quite sure that he would be most emphatic about the timing and manner in which they would meet the guests. Once the party had started his every move would be done with a specific purpose in mind and carried out with a precision that would make any Centurion proud.

"You are breathtaking!" Cornelius gasped when he saw her enter the room. "I see your mother has given you the necklace I gave her on the evening that I asked her to be my wife. You are almost as beautiful as she was on that night."

"Thank you, Father."

"Are you ready?" he asked.

"I am ready and I hope I do not disappoint you," replied Niccoli.

"You have never disappointed me," Cornelius declared and smiled as he led her to the back of the curtains that were expressly hung to create the proper effect for their grand entrance.

Niccoli placed her hand upon the back of Cornelius' hand and he gently held her fingertips with his thumb and forefinger. He straightened his arm out in front of himself and threw back his shoulders in final preparation for the moment they would greet their guests. After an approving look at his daughter, he took a deep breath and gestured for the trumpets to sound their grand entrance. At the sound of the trumpets, a hush fell over the guests and all eyes focused upon the curtains as they parted to reveal the host and hostess. A gasp of adoration and awe rippled throughout the room as they gazed upon the couple.

Cornelius stood straight and proud before them and radiated an air of importance and grandeur. Even in his elder years he was a handsome man and looked flamboyant in his cream-colored tunic that was embellished with jewels set in the midst of golden embroidered swirls that bordered the neckline.

Niccoli, as promised, had woven roses, wild flowers and

pearl accents throughout her hair. The light of many candles lit the room and reflected in the gems around her neck. Each breath that she took made the stones glisten with a brilliance that only stones of that magnitude could reflect. The light behind her softly filtered through the multi-layered silk dress and accentuated her flawless figure.

A thunderous round of applause and cheers rose up from the guests, and Cornelius, pleased with their response, smiled and nodded a recognition to each as he moved forward down the aisle that the trumpeters had formed. He enjoyed every minute of the glorious fanfare and played his role to the utmost.

Niccoli walked beside her father and smiled as she passed the Roman elite. She hated their pompous ways with all of her heart but remained a gracious hostess, wanting only to please her father. She stayed at his side while he made the rounds of greetings and introductions. She graciously smiled at the babbling, insincere and often times obese men who always seemed insistent upon kissing her hand or taking a stolen pinch.

"Niccoli, I know you are bored with this scene, but before you leave my side I would like for you to meet the young centurion standing by the wine table. He not only is looked upon with favor but he is intelligent and very handsome. Perhaps he can whisk you away from all of this. I am sure you would rather be with someone who is closer to your age," Cornelius whispered through a smile that was meant for the others in the room.

"Father, please," Niccoli begged, "I do not wish to meet anyone, much less one of Nero's boys."

"You never mind," Cornelius coaxed, patting her hand as he spoke. "I am sure you will find him quite interesting." Ignoring her protest he quickly maneuvered her to the wine table and stopped in front of the centurion.

"Ah, my friend," Cornelius greeted with a flare, "I am

impressed for I see you have found the best wine in the room. Please allow me the honor of introducing my daughter. Niccoli, this is Damon. He has managed to impress my colleagues and, as you well know, that is not an easy accomplishment. Damon...my daughter."

Her father was right. Damon was strikingly handsome. His dark hair, dark eyes, and flashing smile instantly took her off guard. She observed his muscular stature and thought that he was indeed the perfect example of what a Centurion should look like. She blushed a slight bit at what she was thinking and focused back into the now and realized that he was speaking to her.

"Your father has told me of his daughter and her beauty," he was saying, "but he did not do you justice." As he spoke he bowed and kissed her hand. "You are far more beautiful than he had ever described."

'Oh, please,' Niccoli thought to herself, 'not more false flattery.'

"Cornelius, with your permission I would like to capture your daughter and relieve her from this boring round of introductions."

"By all means," Cornelius responded. "Go, help yourselves to the feast and more wine."

Damon offered Niccoli his arm and she accepted graciously. "Your father has outdone himself again," Damon noted.

"You have been to his festivities before?" Niccoli asked.

"Yes, on two other occasions, but where has he been hiding you for all of this time?"

"I am here tonight in place of my mother," Niccoli answered. "She could not make it this evening. I do not care for such huge affairs."

"Then we have at least one thing in common," stated Damon.

Niccoli only smiled. She did not wish to reveal any

particulars about herself because she considered him to be the enemy, even though he was charming and handsome.

"You are very elusive. Do I frighten you?" Damon asked.

"Somewhat. Have you tried the fowl?" Niccoli replied, trying to change the subject. "I understand it is quite good."

"Oh, I see. You are changing the subject." Damon laughed.

"No, of course not. I was only trying to be a good hostess." Niccoli replied coyly.

"Yes, I have tasted the fowl and it is very good," Damon answered, playing along with the game. "Don't you think that it is stuffy in here? Far too many people standing around! With your permission, I'll get you a goblet of wine and then we can escape to the courtyard and get a breath of clean air."

"That would be refreshing," Niccoli agreed, then added in a teasing manner, "will I be safe alone with you? Does a centurion have impeccable manners?"

"As safe as you wish to be," replied Damon with a twinkle in his deep brown eyes.

"Then I have nothing to fear," Niccoli acknowledged. "I shall meet you in the courtyard."

The cool night air was indeed refreshing and Niccoli took a deep breath to rid her lungs of the stuffy, indecorous air she was forced to breath while inside. How could her father enjoy it so?

Damon, returning with the wine, stopped for a moment in the columned archway to admire the striking silhouette that Niccoli's body created against the starlit sky. Taken by her beauty, he was very interested in getting to know her better.

"Your wine," he spoke softly, not wanting to startle her.

"Thank you," she said with a smile as she took the goblet from his hand. She nodded towards the festivities before continuing, "I am grateful to you for rescuing me. I needed to get away from all of that."

"It is I that should be grateful. I was all too glad for the distraction that you afforded me," replied Damon. "I find these types of engagements boring but necessary. I must deal with them far too many times to suit me. I came tonight out of duty."

"Duty?" quizzed Niccoli.

"Come now, you are a Senator's daughter. You know the politics that are involved in the parliament."

"I try to stay as far away from politics as possible," Niccoli replied with a firmness that surprised Damon.

"But, you are a Senator's daughter."

"I was born a Senator's daughter. I love my father very much, of that you can be assured, and I am loyal to him beyond question. However, I know that I would never choose his profession if I had been a son."

"Well spoken, and just what would you choose?"

"It does not matter," replied Niccoli.

"Perhaps not for a woman. It matters a great deal to a man," Damon affirmed.

"I am sure that it does."

Damon appeared deep in thought as he started drawing aimlessly with his toe in the dirt beside the marble court-yard.

"Are you now bored with me?" Niccoli finally asked when some time had passed.

"By all means, no," Damon insisted. "I am only trying very hard to understand you."

"Understand me?" questioned Niccoli.

"Tell me, how would you react if I put my life in your hands?" asked Damon as he rose to look Niccoli in the eyes.

"What could you possibly do that would cause your life to be in my hands?" Niccoli was quite surprised by his statement.

"This," he said and without hesitation he drew the upper portion of a fish in the dirt and watched for Niccoli's reaction.

"You?" questioned Niccoli with a start. Her heart quickened and she felt frightened. Was this a trick? "How can you be Christian and a Centurion at the same time? You are joking, of course."

"I am quite serious," Damon said with conviction. "So, you do recognize the sign. I thought perhaps you might."

"I recognize it only because of the time that I spent in Jerusalem," Niccoli stated. "Is this some kind of a trap? I assure you there is no reason for you to be testing me."

Quite the contrary. I am looking for fellow Christians. I think it is possible to praise the God of Jesus and still serve in the defense of Rome."

"What makes you think that I know something about this God of Jesus? From what I have heard he is an enemy of Rome," responded Niccoli.

"He is not an enemy of mine," confirmed Damon.

"Perhaps not. But I do not want to get involved," answered Niccoli. "It is getting late. Please excuse me. I must tell my guests good evening. Meeting you has been quite interesting, however, you must be more careful to whom you speak of Jesus. Perhaps I am a spy."

Niccoli smiled and turned toward her other guests, leaving Damon wondering what had just happened.

CHAPTER 13

Niccoli had taken a special interest in lepers and their plight since her contact with the leper on the day Jesus had healed her. She had made it a habit to do weekly visits at the leper colonies, both in Jerusalem and now in Rome. Granted, there was not much that she could do for them, but she offered encouragement and tried to make them as comfortable as possible. Today, however, something made her stop and take a closer look at a woman on the ground beside her. "Lydia, is it you!" she gasped as she knelt beside the mother of Helena, her childhood friend. She was shocked to see that the leprosy had eaten away at her flesh to the point that she had lost many of her facial features.

"Oh, Niccoli," responded Lydia. Her brow, knitted with deep burrows, relaxed a bit and a smile came across her face when she realized who had spoken to her. "How many years has it been since you played with my Helena?"

"Quite a few," answered Niccoli. "I am so sorry to find you here in this place."

"Yes, well...one never knows what life has in store for them."

"How true," replied Niccoli, "so tell me, how is Helena?"

"I have no idea, I have not heard from her for years," Lydia confided." "Her ostracism hurt me deeply and at first I did not think I could go on without her in my life. But, as you can see, I am still here. Life can sometimes be cruel. I think that it was too hard for Helena to see me because then she would have to acknowledge the fact that her mother is a leper."

"How horrible!" sympathized Niccoli, thinking there was very little worse than to be shunned by her family. "How have you managed to cope with all of this?"

"I remained sane only through the grace of God, and the love of Jesus, my Saviour," explained Lydia.

"You know my Jesus?" asked Niccoli, surprised to find a believer in the leper colony.

"Oh yes, I took Him as my Saviour years ago when I saw Him in Jerusalem." Lydia's voice cracked with emotion. "I had gone there to visit Pontius Pilate and his family, and was present when they crucified Him. I saw Him hang upon that cross, and when He died I saw the heavens grow dark and the ground open up!"

"Lydia! I was also there!" declared Niccoli.

"You were? Oh, Niccoli, to have met Him was such a privilege."

"Yes," affirmed Niccoli.

"I have loved Him ever since the short time that I was in Jerusalem. I saw how His miracles made the blind to see, and the crippled to walk tall and straight again. He has been my sustenance ever since and, even though I am a leper, it is because of Him that I have a reason to live. This place, horrible as it is, has given me the opportunity to share His love with the people around me who are desperate and without hope."

"You are a true believer!" confirmed Niccoli, and then she turned very somber. "You have heard how Nero is killing the Christians here in Rome? I doubt that he cares what happens here in the colony, but the Christians on the outside must be extremely careful. We have been forced to go underground for our gatherings."

"Yes, I have heard," replied Lydia sadly. "If we have nothing else in this forsaken place, we do have a very good communication system. There is little of the outside that we do not know. Tell me, where are you staying?"

"At the home of my father. I returned from Jerusalem to help the Christians here in Rome and to care for my Mother who is quite ill."

"I am sorry to hear that your mother is ill, and you are a good daughter to come back and care for her. But Niccoli, you must be very careful about who you trust," cautioned Lydia.

"Yes, I am very aware of that. I certainly do not feel safe on the streets and I am always looking over my shoulder, however, I do feel I have some refuge in my father's home. The Roman soldiers would not dare enter his dwelling and accuse me of wrong doing."

"Do not be too sure," warned Lydia. "The Roman government is very devious, and when they want something they will get it with no thought to anyone that stands in their way. I sense that you are in grave danger, Niccoli."

"I hope that you are wrong," replied a solemn Niccoli, for she could not deny the nagging feeling that Lydia could very easily be correct. "Please do not worry about me, you have enough worries of your own. I must leave now, but I will return."

"Take care, my Niccoli."

When Niccoli arrived home she was surprised to see Cornelius standing in the courtyard. Why had he arrived home so early in the day? Her immediate thought was that something had happened to her mother. "Mother! Is she alright?" she cried.

"Your mother is fine. It is you that is the cause for my early return home!" shouted Cornelius as he approached her and pointed his finger in her face. "Niccoli, how many times do I have to tell you to stay away from that filthy leper colony?"

He not only was extremely angry with her for again deliberately disobeying his order, but also deeply concerned and frustrated about how he could stop her from associating with the lepers?

"Father, were you having me followed?" she snapped back. "How else would you know that I have been to the leper colony?"

"No, of course not!" Cornelius yelled. He respected her more than that, even though he knew that he could not trust her where the lepers were concerned. "One of the soldiers saw you and reported to me, otherwise I would not have known that you had disobeyed me again. Tell me, why do you feel such an attraction to those horrible leper outcasts? Do you want to be one of them? You know that I could not protect you if you became infected! Oh, Niccoli, I could not bear the thought of you living in that disgusting filth along side the rest of the lepers. Please listen to reason," pleaded Cornelius.

"God is watching over me," replied Niccoli, "because I have been with lepers for many years now. I was helping them when I was in Jerusalem and I have not yet come down with the disease. Do not worry so." She hoped that her reasoning would convince her father that he need not worry, but her efforts were unsuccessful and her reasoning fell on deaf ears.

"Niccoli, I order you, do not go again!"

"Father, please listen to me," pleaded Niccoli, trying hard to appeal to his nurturing side, "did you know that Helena's mother is in the colony? Her entire family has abandoned her and she has no one to comfort her. I can not turn my back on her."

"Her daughter had the sense to!" he shouted and then softened. "Niccoli, I am very sorry for her, but that is not your problem. I do not want you there with her. It is as simple as that!"

"Father, I am sorry, I know how concerned you are, but I can not promise that I will never go to the colony again.

Someone has to be concerned about the lepers' problems and I know that I can be of some comfort to them."

Several weeks went by and, out of respect for her father; she had not gone to the leper colony. This morning, however, something was pulling at her heart, and she could not get Lydia out of her mind. She had learned from past experiences that when she felt this way she must follow her instincts; knowing that God was leading her to do His will. Even though she did not always understand His plan, she knew that she needed to be obedient and follow His lead without question. Not wanting to awaken her father, she got out of bed and dressed as quickly and quietly as she could. Surprisingly, she managed to slip undetected out the front door into the crisp and beautiful morning air.

She walked at a brisk pace and was well aware of every moving thing around her even though it was relatively quiet; few people were walking the streets at that early hour. It did not take long to arrive at the gate of the leper colony, and, as she entered and surveyed the lepers lying on the ground all around her, she felt so sorry that most did not have beds or mats to lie upon nor blankets to cover with. She did not readily see Lydia and gingerly stepped over the sleeping disfigured bodies, stopping periodically to stoop down and take a closer look at a particular face. Where was she? Why couldn't she find her? Then, out of the quiet, she heard her name.

"Niccoli, is that you?" Lydia's voice was just a whisper and barely audible.

"Lydia, I was so worried," replied Niccoli as she hurried over and knelt beside her. "When I could not find you, I was beginning to think I would never see you again. I am so sorry I have not visited you sooner but father gets so upset when I come. I do try to respect his wishes whenever I can, but today was different! When I awoke this morning I could not get you out of my mind, and I had to come see you. Are you alright?"

"I have been feeling rather poorly these last few days," replied Lydia.

"I am so sorry," sympathized Niccoli, "I wish I could ease the pain that you feel."

"I am sure that you do, Niccoli. It is only that the mornings have been rather cold as of late."

"I brought you some soup. If you can sit up, I'll feed you." Niccoli said as she took Lydia in her arms.

Lydia smiled at Niccoli, attempted to eat a few spoonfuls, but soon pushed the spoon away. "I thank you for your concern," she said in a weak voice, "but I am very tired, and I would like to lie down now."

"I wish you would eat more," coaxed Niccoli, but Lydia just closed her eyes and shook her head ever so slightly. Niccoli smiled and gently eased her friend's mother back down to the ground. Suddenly, Lydia was surrounded with a golden light that beamed down upon her from the heavens. It was so brilliant that Niccoli had to shield her eyes. Then, just as she thought it could not be any brighter, it changed to an all encompassing, sparkling white glow, that pulsated. Lydia's face was radiant as she broke into a smile, and Niccoli realized that her friend was looking at something, or somebody, that was not being revealed to her. "Lydia, what is happening?" she asked, but there was no response.

Long after the white light had vanished, Lydia's countenance still glowed and a most peaceful look was upon her face as she quietly absorbed the experience. Niccoli had never seen anything like it before. She could feel herself trembling as she waited, rather impatiently, for Lydia to speak.

"Niccoli, Jesus was just here. Did you see Him?"

"No, all I saw was a magnificent light."

"Niccoli, He spoke to me. Did you hear Him? He said that on this day I would join Him in heaven."

Niccoli caught her breath and tears whelmed in her eyes.

"Oh, do not be sad!" Lydia said, wanting Niccoli to join

her in her jubilation, "Be joyful. This is the most beautiful day of my life!"

"I am sorry for being so selfish in wanting you to stay," Niccoli sobbed.

"Who would have ever guessed it," Lydia whispered, and then fell extremely quiet.

"Lydia, are you alright?" Niccoli asked, but there was no response. "Lydia, do you hear me?" she shook her gently but there was still no response. "Oh, Lydia," Niccoli sobbed, "save a place for me at Jesus' side."

She cupped Lydia in her arms and rocked her until she felt cold to the touch. She wondered what had happened to the blanket that she had given Lydia and looked around to see if she could find it. There, huddled in a corner she saw a woman wrapped in it who was watching her every move with curious eyes. "Please," Niccoli said to her, "would you give me your blanket so that I can cover my friend's dead body?"

"No, it is the only blanket that I have," was the reply. "Why do you fuss so? She is dead! Leave her alone! They will come in time and take the body to the leper's burial ground."

"I do not want her to be buried there! I am taking her to my burial plot," declared Niccoli. "I just want to cover her body until I return for her. Lend me your blanket and I promise you that I will bring you a new blanket."

"No!"

"Is there anyone here among you that will loan me their blanket until I can bring them a new one?" pleaded Niccoli. After a long silence a woman slowly crept forward.

"Here is mine, please take it and cover her. She was so good to me during the time that she was here, and I wish to do something for her."

"God bless you."

"That is exactly what she always said to me."

"Sir," Niccoli asked of a man standing near, "would you help me carry her closer to the gate so that my servants will be able to retrieve her upon my return."

"Why are you doing this? Why are you here?" he asked. "Do you not know that we are outcasts?"

"Yes, I am aware of that, but I am here because my heart goes out to you, and I want to help in any way I can. This disease does not single out the poor or the evil; it can attack any one of us. For instance, this woman was the mother of my childhood friend of long ago and I can not turn my back upon her now."

Without another word the man stooped down, scooped Lydia into his arms, and carried her to the gate. "I will stand guard over her until you return," he promised and placed her gently on the ground close to him.

"Thank you," said Niccoli, "you will be awarded in heaven."

'Yes,' she thought to herself as she looked down at Lydia, 'no matter what life has in store for us, there is always a way to glorify our Lord!'

Niccoli hurried home and called two of her most trusted men servants to her side. "Come," she said, "I need the two of you to go with me to the leper colony and pick up a dear friend who has just died. We will take her body to my family's burial plot and prepare a place for her to be buried there." She laughed to herself at what her father's reaction would be if he found out a leper was buried near him. "My father would be quite upset if he knew what we are doing, so we must bury her at the edge of our plot and in a place that will be inconspicuous to my father. I give you warning, you will be subject to his wrath as well as I, and so this must remain our secret. Do you understand fully what I have said to you?"

"Yes, we understand. But do you understand our concern? We do not want to touch her. What if we get her leprosy?" asked the braver of the servants. "I speak for myself and the others, we do not want to take the risk of handling her."

"Do as you are told!" scolded Niccoli but then added. "I have been with lepers for years and I am not infected. If it will make you feel better to cover yourself and bind your arms and hands, then do so. I give my permission for you to burn your clothes when you get home. I will purchase your new clothes out of my allowance. Now, come with me, time is wasting and Lydia's body will not wait. Remember, neither Father nor Mother can know of this."

Niccoli hated to deceive her father, but knew if he had knowledge of what she was doing he would go into a rage. She reasoned it would be much better to spare him of that 'potential health hazard'.

CHAPTER 14

D amon could not get Niccoli out of his mind. She was breathtaking; charming but yet aloof, beautiful but not vain, and rich beyond most dreams but not a snob. She was everything a man could ask for, and she would not even give him a second glance. He had the distinct feeling that she did not trust him and wondered why; what could he have done to make her feel so distrustful? He did not understand, but the one thing he knew for sure was that he had to see her again.

He mulled over the various ways to ask her out, and decided that a 'mock kidnapping' would be most fun and different. He would take her to his favorite spot in the country, which would be far away from the busy streets of Rome and the prying eyes of the elite.

"Geno, get my horse ready," he called to his servant. "Tell the others to immediately prepare a lunch for two. I have important business to attend to."

He freshened himself and put on his brightest gold mantle. "Hurry," he ordered, when the servants had not yet brought his horse and lunch to him. "I do not have all day to wait on you!"

"Yes, master," Geno, responded as he hastened to bridle the horse. "We have everything ready for you."

Sandra S. Jones

"Excellent!" he shouted out as he mounted his white charger and took the basket that Geno held out to him. "Wish me luck, Geno!" He sped off at top speed to rescue his lady from what he imagined to be boredom without him.

By the time he had arrived at the home of Cornelius, he was starting to have second thoughts. Had he acted too hastily? What if she would not see him, or even worse, send him away with a threat of what she would do if he ever came back. He was sitting on his horse, contemplating what he should do, when the door opened and he saw Niccoli walking towards him.

"Damon, why are you at my front door?" she asked.

Damon, surprised by her sudden appearance, managed to stutter, "To see you."

"Really," she teased. "And just how long were you planning to stay seated on your beautiful horse before seeing me?"

Damon was embarrassed. No other woman had ever affected him this way, nor had they ever caught him off guard as she had just managed to do. "Actually," he said with newly found authority, "I have come to kidnap you and take you to the most beautiful spot that you can imagine." He held up the lunch basket and continued, "See, I have even brought a lunch for us to share."

"How nice, but what if I have already eaten?"

"Have you?" he queried, disappointment evident in his voice.

"Well...no," she said coyly.

"Wonderful!" he exclaimed. "Then we are off!" He bent down, took her by the arm and pulled her up behind him on the horse's back.

"I cannot ride this way," she protested.

"Why not? I promise you, it will be one of the most exciting things you have ever done," he said. Making sure that she was in place behind him, he kicked the horse and it bolted into a full run. "Put your arms around my waist and

176 ·

hold on tight!"

"Damon!" she cried out, but she was barely audible as her voice trailed off in the wind that passed by her.

As they raced through the streets Niccoli's hair blew straight out behind her, and her long flowing dress came to rest above her thighs as she sat with one leg on either side of the horse. She wanted Damon to stop, but she was so breathless she could not speak.

Soon they were out of the city and Damon slowed the horse to a trot. "Thank you," Niccoli managed to say. "It is about time that you slowed down. Has anyone told you that you're reckless?"

"Admit it, you loved the ride!"

Niccoli laughed, "I will admit to nothing!"

"Niccoli," Damon teased as he helped her down. "I had a suspicion that you loved spontaneity and now, at this very moment, as I look at your face I am sure of it. You love the excitement of doing the unexpected!"

"Well, I have to admit it was a thrilling ride," she laughed as she straightened her hair and clothes. "Also very unladylike. I hope word does not get back to my father."

"They would not have believed their eyes even if they had seen you. I am sure your father will never know," he assured her.

Damon walked over to the tree that stood in the middle of the meadow and picked a nice shady spot to spread the blanket. "Here, come sit and rest yourself," he coaxed. "I know you must be tired from all that excitement."

"Please, spare me," she replied. "I have a lot of breath left in me."

"I am sure that you do," laughed Damon, "nevertheless, I bet you are hungry."

"Perhaps a little," was the reply.

"Good, let's see what my servants have prepared for us. Yes," he exclaimed with enthusiasm and lifted up a bottle of

wine for Niccoli to see. "A bottle of my best wine. I hope cheese, dates and bread are to your liking."

"Sounds wonderful!"

Damon took a sip of the wine and leaned back on his elbow as he watched Niccoli take a sip. "You are very exciting!" he said.

"Do not flatter me any more, or I will think that you are only trying to get your way with me."

"I am sorry, I would not insult you in that way," he assured her. He studied her as she ate and sipped the wine. "Tell me, how long have you been back in Rome?" he asked.

"I see you have been checking up on me."

"No, it is common knowledge that you were studying in Jerusalem."

"I have been back for awhile."

"Why did you come back?" he quizzed.

"My mother is critically ill," was the response.

"Is that the only reason?" he asked as he pulled off a piece of cheese and sipped more wine.

"Why do you ask such a question?" Niccoli asked, and immediately she put up her defense.

"Do not get upset, I was only wondering if there was some other reason that caused your return. Possibly a man?"

"May God wash out your mouth," laughed Niccoli. "My father is the only man in my life."

"Thank goodness. I am not up to competition."

"I am sure," Niccoli bantered. "I do not feel that you are very convincing."

Damon just shrugged his shoulders and then lay back on the wool blanket. He looked up at the sky and noticed dark clouds starting to gather in the west. "I hate to bring a halt to such a great time," he commented, "but look, it is going to storm. Perhaps we should pack our things and start back to the city."

They had barely gathered things together when it started

to sprinkle, and by the time they were mounted on the horse it had become a downpour. Niccoli could not believe it; first she was racing through the streets of Rome in a most undignified manner, and now, she would be returning looking like a drowned rodent. What a day to remember!

Damon sought out every excuse imaginable just to see Niccoli and to be near her. Whenever he could manage the time from his duties he would take her on jaunts out to the country, or squeeze in long walks in the evenings. He knew that she had let down her defenses and was becoming more comfortable with him when she told him about some of her experiences in Jerusalem. She told of how she had been witness to the crucifixion of Jesus and how she had seen Him on the day of His resurrection.

Damon wanted to bind their friendship and love together with something special and had searched everywhere for a gift that would be appropriate for her, but nothing measured up. It was some time before he thought of giving her something that was fashioned by his own hand, and remembering how touched she was by the crucifixion, he decided to whittle a small cross for her to hang hidden around her neck. He searched for an olive branch that would be perfect for what he envisioned in his mind, and was now appreciative for the time that he had spent as a young child learning the art of whittling from his grandfather. He hoped that the training was going to be sufficient to fashion a perfect cross. Only the best would be good enough for Niccoli, and anything that he would fashion had to be absolutely perfect.

Taking the branch in his hand, he sighted down it as he turned it to determine where to start forming the cross with the figure of the dying man. The thickest part of the branch seemed promising, but he still had to decide if the grain would be acceptable. 'Yes, it should do just fine,' he decided.

He cut away the excess portions and, keeping the vision

in his mind, worked with loving and precise strokes as he guided his knife across the now smooth olive branch. More than anything else he wanted to gain favor in Niccoli's eyes. It was his fervent wish that she would accept the cross and appreciate the fact that it had been fashioned especially for her by his own hand.

He knew that he had to be careful and not let anyone know what he was doing. If any of the other centurions saw the cross they would immediately report him to Nero and he would risk the chance of being killed along with the other Christians.

There were chips of wood all around him when a knock at the door interrupted his whittling. He hurriedly hid the creation under a blanket that was on the divan nearby and swept the chips under the mat next to the chair in which he was sitting. Satisfied that there were no tattle-tail traces of what he was doing, he opened the door.

"Damon, Nero has requested an audience with you," the messenger said with an air of importance in his voice. "He wants me to escort you there without hesitation."

"Well, then, what are we waiting for? Let us not keep Nero waiting!" Damon replied lightheartedly.

The messenger gave Damon a quick look of disgust. To be called for an audience with Nero was not something to take so lightly.

Damon noticed the look and chided, "Do not take things so seriously." He slapped the messenger on the shoulder and continued. "It will cause you to grow old much sooner than your time."

Disgruntled, the messenger fetched his horse and waited just outside the door in readiness for Damon. When Damon finally mounted his horse, he gave an arrogant smile to the messenger and dug his heels deep into the horse's belly. He held himself erect as the horse reared and pawed the air, and the moment its hoofs hit the ground again the horse took off with a speed equaled by no other. Damon yelled with delight as his horse sped down the crowded Roman streets with the messenger in close pursuit. They did not care that the people had to scramble to get out of the way of their spirited horses; knowing full well that the people could be trampled to death. Oblivious to his surroundings Damon and the messenger sped onward without even a backward glance.

As they approached Nero's palace, the guards recognized Damon and bowed to him, lowered their spears and opened the gates. Damon acknowledged gestures of greeting from all he met. The statement Cornelius had made to his daughter regarding the fact that Damon was held high in Nero's favor was obvious throughout the court.

Damon stopped at the base of the steps leading to the palace, and the steward took the reins of his horse so that he could dismount. Muscles in his arms flexed as he lowered himself to the ground. Without hesitation he quickly climbed the steps and made his way to the throne room; the inner guards bowed their heads in recognition, and respectfully opened the door to allow Damon admittance.

"Hail, Nero!" Damon greeted in a loud clear voice as he hit his chest with his fist in the proper salute to Nero.

Nero quietly studied Damon and made a slight gesture with his hand that gave him permission to approach the throne. "I expected to see you sooner," he said. The sarcasm and irritation were evident in his voice as he continued. "Is there some unforeseen problem I know nothing about? Or perhaps you have allowed yourself the luxury of becoming too involved with your assigned subject and it has clouded your reasoning?"

"I am loyal to you to the end, Great Nero. You know that I have never allowed anything to come between my assigned duty or you. It just takes time to lay the groundwork in a proper and discreet manner. I am being extremely careful to see that my objective is not discovered. I promise that it will not be long before you will be proud to have me at your side in absolute victory," Damon assured Nero.

"Be sure that the victory is ours and not theirs. How I do detest those Christians. They make my skin crawl."

"Without question, mighty Nero," Damon responded.

"Leave. Report back at the first sign of victory," Nero said and dismissed Damon by turning his back and motioning for the wine steward.

Damon bowed and took his leave. In his heart he knew Nero could turn on him just as quickly as he could blink an eye, so he had to quicken his attack. The groundwork was prepared and now it was necessary to get the attack started. In a way, what he had to do to accomplish his assignment saddened him, and he knew he had to concentrate on how great the rewards would be to keep himself focused. Otherwise, he would not have the heart to continue.

'Fat pompous pig,' Damon thought to himself as he made his exit. He despised Nero and all that he stood for. More times than not he hated the duties assigned to him, and this assignment was the most distasteful. He knew, however, that he had to maintain rapport with his superior if he wanted to advance in the ranks of the Roman army.

His thoughts went back to the cross that he was carving for Niccoli. He wanted to win her favor just as much as he wanted his career to be successful, and he hoped it would be something that would impress her. If he hurried, perhaps it would be feasible to finish it that night.

He worked long into the night and decided that the cross was one of his best carvings, a fact for which he was grateful. The following morning he hurried to Cornelius' home to see Niccoli. The morning was beautiful and the air was crisp as he rode up on his beautiful white mare. She was his prized possession and he was proud of the way she pranced in grand style. When she raced through the street it gave him a sense of power to watch the people scatter to get out of his way.

Upon his arrival, the servant took him to the garden where Niccoli was sitting, busily piecing together a wall hanging. She looked up and smiled at her suitor as he approached. She was more than fond of him and welcomed his arrival.

Damon gave her a boyish grin and bowed low. "Peace be with you," he said.

"And with you," she replied.

"It is so good to see you," replied Damon as he knelt beside her. "I wish I could capture the beauty of you sitting before me now."

"You flatter me more than I deserve."

"Not nearly enough," replied Damon. "I have missed you. When I am away from you, every minute seems like an hour."

Niccoli could feel her face flush and felt her heart beat rapidly in her ears. She hoped that he would not notice the extent to which he excited her.

Damon took the cross from his pocket and put it in her hand. He closed her fingers over it and sat back upon his heels to wait for her reaction.

Niccoli looked down and opened her hand. Her eyes widened and a gasp escaped from her lips. She was surprised to see the carved cross with the figure of Jesus hanging upon it. The detailed work was astounding. "It is beautiful!" she whispered. "Did you carve this?"

"Yes, my grandfather taught me to whittle many years ago. I am now more grateful to him than ever before because it has given me great joy to be able to fashion this for you. I hope that it is to your liking."

"Oh Damon...it is so lovely! Thank you, I will cherish it always," Niccoli said as she clutched the cross to her bosom. "I only wish I could wear it on a chain around my neck for all to see. Perhaps I will be able to do so in the near future."

"Perhaps some day you will," Damon replied.

Niccoli stood up and Damon put his arms around her. He held her close as their lips met. She was so responsive to his

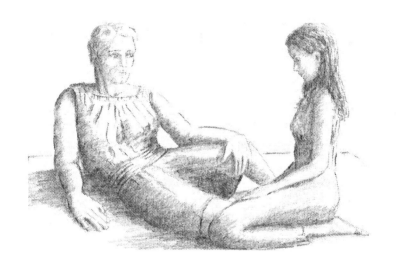

touch, that he felt a lump in his stomach and knew that he must release her before he did something that he would later regret.

"Do you have some wine?" he asked. "I am very thirsty from my ride over."

"Yes, of course, and I have been such a bad hostess," Niccoli replied and clapped her hands to signal her servant. "Please bring us some of Father's best wine," she ordered. "I have just received a most wonderful gift and I want to celebrate."

"Yes, we do need to celebrate," declared Damon as he again took her into his arms. "Niccoli, I want to share my life with you, to share our innermost secrets and leave nothing out."

Niccoli looked up at him through tears that were now streaming down her cheeks. All the struggles and fears of the times melted away, and joy enveloped her as she felt the arms of the man she loved around her. She listened to Damon proclaim his love for her and for the first time she dropped all of her defenses and allowed herself to be swept into the wonderful essence of love.

Together they sipped wine and talked long into the night, sharing their secrets and plans for the future. His openness and charm made her feel as though she had known him forever. Their paths in time had just not crossed until now.

"Niccoli, you have one more thing to share with me," Damon whispered.

"Really, I thought I had shared all of my inner most secrets."

"Well, yes, but I feel that you don't trust me enough to share the Christian organizational meetings with me?" Damon confessed, the emotion in his voice was quite evident. "I know that I am a new convert, and have many things to learn, but it would mean so much to me. Plus, I feel that you are leaving me out of the most important part of your life. Tonight we talked of plans for the future, but there cannot be a future unless you include me in everything. Don't you trust me enough to share them with me?"

"Oh, Damon," replied Niccoli, "of course I trust you. I would trust you with my life if need be. I am sorry, I am so use to protecting my Christian friends that I did not realize I was leaving you out of something you wanted so badly. Yes, of course, you may come to the next meeting with me."

"Good, you have made me feel much better," replied Damon with a sigh of relief. He was now satisfied that she would share everything with him.

Niccoli told him about her Christian friends and the meetings that she and Andrew conducted. She cried softly when she told him how saddened she was that Nero persecuted the Christians, and stated that it was beyond her understanding why he would do such a thing. How could he feel threatened by a group of people who were gentle by nature and did no wrong to others?

Damon held Niccoli in his arms and listened intently to her every word. He had finally won her confidence and trust as well as her love.

CHAPTER 15

Niccoli felt that she had finally found the man she had always searched for. One who excited her, challenged her very being, and shared her love for Jesus. Damon's interest in the Christian movement had created an even greater common bond between them and she felt that he loved her in the deepest sense of the word. He accepted her for the person she was, not because she was a Senator's daughter or a beautiful dancer. Instead he saw her as a woman who loved without restraints and asked for nothing but love in return.

When they were together he either held her hand or had his arm around her, making her feel as though he was saying to the world: 'This is my woman and I will protect her.' Tonight, however, he was especially quiet as they walked hand in hand in the moonlight. After a long silence he stopped, and she could see the troubled look he had on his face as he looked down at her.

"Niccoli," he started, his voice barely audible. "I am not good for you, nor am I worthy of your love. I can never give you the love you deserve."

"Shhhh," she replied as she put her finger to his lips signaling him to say no more. "I am just happy being with you and I love you as you are. Do not speak words of unworthiness that will spoil this moment," she said as she stretched to kiss his cheek.

Damon drew her close and Niccoli's heart sang with songs of love as she totally lost herself in his embrace. She thrilled at his touch, never before had she loved someone so totally. She felt she could share her innermost thoughts freely with him and never be condemned for the views or emotions that she felt. He gently took her chin in his hand and lifted her face so he could kiss her lips. When they met it was as though the world stood still and nothing else had any meaning. The only thing that was real was the oneness they felt together.

"Niccoli, you are so trusting and open," he continued, his voice quivering with emotion. "I could never again find anyone else like you. I love holding you in my arms and feeling your body pressed close to mine. Every fiber in my body aches for more, but it can never be. I cannot give what you expect from me. I am so sorry."

Niccoli was stunned. She lifted her head from its resting place upon his chest and looked up at his face. She did not understand what was happening. She tried to absorb the meaning of his words but she was so confused. "What are you saying?" she questioned.

"I must leave you now. Besides, you need to get some rest, for you have been pushing yourself much too hard." He gave her a quick kiss on the forehead and a loving pat on her back before he released her. "Goodbye, my sweet innocent lamb," he muttered as he turned his back, mounted his horse and rode away.

Niccoli was in shock, standing alone and longing for more. He had jolted her by his quick goodbye and non-committal attitude. She had heard his words but did not understand their meaning. The only thing she was confident of was that she wanted to be with him always, but now, suddenly, he indicated that he did not want the same. She sensed a great divide between them that she had never felt before. Why? What had caused this change in him?

"Goodbye, my love," she whispered as she watched him leave.

Damon also was disturbed over their meeting. He knew that Niccoli was upset and realized that he had far deeper feelings for her than he ever had intended, however, he was fully aware that he could not permit himself to fall in love with her. He had rigid plans already set for the future and they did not include a life with her. What was happening saddened him but he simply could not allow her to get any closer to him. His plans were more important to him and the decision had already been made; he had to do what was asked of him.

Niccoli stood alone in the garden for some time before she went inside to check on her mother. In the past year Niccoli had watched her mother become very frail and, even though her mother received the best of care from the servants, Niccoli liked to pamper her and make sure she was as comfortable as possible. It was rewarding to see how much it pleased her mother for her to be near.

Even though Niccoli knew Jesus was with her always, she could not help but wish that He was standing in the flesh beside her mother now. She was confident that her mother would be healed with just a touch of His hand.

It was well past midnight before Niccoli had a chance to say her prayers and turn in for the night. She stretched herself out and snuggled between the covers on the comfortable bed. The security of her father's home allowed her to relax a bit even though she knew that she was not safe anywhere. Her thoughts went to Damon and his earlier behavior, as she tried to figure out what had caused him to become so distant. What had she done to cause it? Was he tired of her now? What was wrong? The questions were still troubling her when she eventually dropped off to sleep.

Cornelius had decided that Diana was too weak to discuss the extreme danger Niccoli had exposed herself to by being active in the Christian Movement. He was not sure if she was aware of the atrocities that Nero was inflicting upon the Christians, but did not want to take any chances of placing her at risk with the knowledge that Niccoli was a follower. Neither did he want her to worry that if Nero, or other members of parliament, knew of Niccoli's Christianity it would mean certain death; either by being made into a human torch for his gardens, or as an unwilling participant in the infamous sport of throwing the Christians to the lions.

In his opinion, it was grossly inhuman how Nero and other Romans could sit in the stands and be filled with excitement while they cheered and enjoyed the spectacle of lions tearing humans limb from limb. It was beyond his comprehension how Nero could be so cruel and heartless as he determined the fate of a Christian's life by the turning of his thumb. Thumbs up they lived, thumbs down they died. The polarity between the cruelty he displayed to the Christians, and the love that Jesus had taught, as well as lived, were as opposite as day is to night.

Suddenly, out of the quiet of the night, Cornelius was jolted by a loud thud against the door. A chill ran down his spine and he needed no explanation as to what was happening. He immediately sprang to his feet, ready to protect his daughter.

"Open the door in the name of Nero, your emperor!" yelled a centurion.

In a matter of seconds Cornelius was at his daughter's side. "You must hide in the root cellar near the servant's quarters," he whispered as he hurriedly gathered together all of Niccoli's personal items in the room.

Niccoli bolted for the root cellar. She heard the thud of a log hitting the front door and knew that it would be only a matter of seconds before the soldiers would force their entry. She could hear her mother's frail voice calling out for her or her father but there was no time to respond; to hesitate meant certain death!

The smell of the damp earth filled her nostrils as she curled into a tight ball so that she could fit into the small cramped hole. The servant quickly threw her belongings in beside her, covered her with a dark cloth, stacked food in front of her and closed the door; leaving Niccoli in total darkness.

Cornelius was unable to reach the front door before the soldiers broke its hinges and the heavy door fell with a crash onto the marble floor. The soldiers stormed into the room and scattered like an army of ants in all directions. He was filled with anger as he watched them ravage throughout his home. "What is the meaning of this?" he demanded. "I am a Roman Senator! By what authority do you have for invading my home?"

"Where is the one named Niccoli?" demanded the ugly tempered centurion. "We know that she is here."

"There is no one living here by that name," replied Cornelius as he tried hard to maintain his composure.

The centurion stared him in the eye. "You do have a daughter by that name, do you not?"

Cornelius nodded his head and added, "She now resides in Jerusalem."

"You lie! She has been seen here!" he screamed as he grabbed Cornelius around the neck and flung him to the floor. "Out of my way, old man. You have no status with me. Your rights were relinquished the minute you housed a Christian."

"Search every corner!" he bellowed out to the soldiers with him. "Check under every piece of furniture! We do not leave here until we have found her!"

The soldiers started tossing furniture and ripping tapestries from the walls in a vain attempt to find a secret passageway. Two soldiers overturned the huge cupboard that stood against the center wall, causing its display of beautiful earthen bowls to shatter as they fell to the floor. Wine spewed out of flasks as the heavy cupboard smashed down upon them.

"I will have your head upon a platter!" yelled Cornelius as he viewed the destruction.

The centurion stood in the middle of the room and ignored Cornelius as his eyes darted about to scan the room for possible hiding places. Satisfied there was no other place to look in the main house, he turned and started for the bedroom wings with Cornelius close behind him. He went from one room to another until he came upon Niccoli's bedroom. Seeing the unmade bed he reeled about in anger. "Who was sleeping in this bed?" he demanded.

"It was I," replied Cornelius in a calm but authoritative voice. "My wife is extremely ill, and I often times sleep in this bed so that I might not disturb her." He returned the centurion's stare and prayed in his heart that his story was believable.

The centurion stood his ground and studied Cornelius. It was doubtful that his source of information was incorrect. Nero had sent spies throughout the city to infiltrate the Christian community and they had reported to him of their whereabouts. His orders had come straight from Nero himself.

Because of the great influence Niccoli and Andrew had upon the followers of Jesus, they now were two of the most sought-after Christians. Above all else, Nero wanted to capture them and reveal them as frauds. He wanted to prove that they were only lowly peasants who had nothing to offer.

Confident that Cornelius would protect his daughter at all costs, and also a little concerned about his influence, the centurion decided to call off the search. He posted a guard at the Senator's front door to make sure that if Niccoli was inside he would soon know of it. She might escape him for the moment, but the game was not yet over. He was not going to give up until he had captured her, the protected Senator's daughter.

Cornelius stood in the doorway and listened as the centurion gave orders for the guard to document everyone who went in and out. He ordered that all be searched so that he would be aware of any messages that might be passed along. Fear squeezed the heart of Cornelius to the point of panic. "Niccoli, my sweet Niccoli, what are we going to do?" he whispered softly to himself. How would he ever be able to get his only child to safety with a guard posted outside at all times?

Hours passed into days as the guard faithfully stood his post outside the home. On occasion, when Cornelius was sure Niccoli was safely hidden, he would offer the guard a small cup of wine. His intention was two-fold: one, he wanted to make the guard comfortable, in the hopes that in time he would relax enough to allow Niccoli the time to escape, two, he wanted to learn how they had obtained the information that she was one of the Christians. Cornelius felt that someone close to either Niccoli or himself was the informant and he wanted to know who that person was. He also wanted answers to the many other questions that were bothering him.

The guard seemed nice enough, just a young boy doing his duty, and he did not seem to have any feelings one way or the other about what was happening to the Christians. However, he was there for a purpose, and left no misunderstanding that he would fulfill his duties at all costs. Periodically, he would wander through the house in search of some clue of Niccoli's whereabouts, but up to this point she had always been well hidden. However, Cornelius always worried about the unexpected even though they were extremely careful not to leave any traces of her presence. He knew that he had to get Niccoli out of the house, but he simply had not yet found a way to accomplish this feat. He knew that it had to be very soon because luck would not follow them indefinitely.

Unknown to Cornelius, the underground was ready to execute their plan for Niccoli's escape. On the morrow, Damon would pretend to be a merchant that was selling bread and stop at his home to give one of the servants a test loaf. The following day he would return and ask to see Cornelius so that they might inquire if the bread was to his liking. At that point the plan was to slip Cornelius a loaf of bread that had poisonous herbs baked into it, and to instruct him on how to serve the guard the tainted bread with the usual afternoon wine. He would explain that the bread was not intended to kill the guard, but to only to make him very ill. When he was preoccupied with his sickness, Damon would sneak Niccoli past him to safety.

The designated morning dawned with the hope of success in the air when Andrew called everyone together for last minute instructions. He wanted to go over the plan one last time and check its every detail. He felt the extreme responsibility for the project because he not only had to worry about freeing Niccoli, but also to assure the safety of the other participants. If one person were to be recognized, the entire group would be in danger. Andrew placed the prepared loaves of bread into a basket and pushed them across the table towards Damon, the one chosen to play the part of the merchant because of his close relationship with Niccoli. "Do you understand fully what you are to do?" Andrew inquired of him. "If you have any doubts or questions about this plan, now is the last opportunity that you have to state them."

"No questions, No doubts," answered Damon. "I am ready and anxious to get started. You know Andrew, her safety means everything to me, and I can not wait to hold her in my arms again."

"Then we are ready," Andrew affirmed.

* * *

Niccoli was never far from the cellar door that was located near the servants' quarters. From her vantage point she could see out the window and today, as she watched people come and go, she was especially wishing that she could be free to take a stroll in the warm sunlight. She felt like a caged animal, and the confinement was beginning to wear on her nerves. She rather absentmindedly watched as a merchant knocked on the neighbor's door, and before long he was talking to the guard posted in front of her father's home. She watched as the guard inspected the loaves and, after exchanging a few pleasantries, she was surprised to see that he had allowed the merchant to come around to the back entry.

Suddenly, Niccoli became alert. Could it be? She took a closer look and her heart began to pound in her chest. Yes! It was Damon! He had come to rescue her! Niccoli motioned for the servant to open the door and, when she saw him standing there before her, she wanted to run into his arms and feel the security that only one lover can give to another. But she refrained, knowing that she dare not be so careless. Instead, she quietly stepped out of the shadows and for a moment they stood gazing into each other's eyes. Niccoli started towards him, but Damon motioned for her to stop. She stood motionless and watched as he gave the servant the bread and explained that he would return on the morrow to see if it was to their liking. He thanked the servant and shot a quick glance at Niccoli before turning to leave. Niccoli watched as he walked away, knowing that her freedom was close at hand and that she would soon be in the arms of the man she loved. She silently praised the Lord for sending her hero to save her.

Everything was going as they had planned, and Damon was extremely pleased as he made his way back to the rendezvous. The guard had no suspicion of any misdoing and had accepted him as a merchant. Damon was confident that when he returned with the tainted bread the guard would not question him. He could feel the adrenaline pumping through his veins; how he loved the excitement of adventure and intrigue!

The next morning Damon's steps were brisk as he turned down the street that led to Cornelius' home. The expectation of tricking the guard made him feel exuberant and so alive. What a game! He could hardly wait to execute the final steps.

Upon arrival the guard recognized him and, as speculated, allowed Damon to go to the back entrance of the home. The servant who answered the door was the one that he had talked with the day before.

"Good day," Damon said cheerfully. "Remember me? I brought the bread yesterday and have returned to see if it was to your liking. May I see your master and inquire of him?"

The servant was hesitant to bother her master with such a trivial matter and stammered, "Well, I am not sure. He is a very busy...." her voice faded away as she turned to listen to the voice behind her.

"Tell the merchant to step inside, I will be happy to answer his question."

Damon recognized Niccoli's voice and watched as she stepped forward. Without taking her gaze off Damon she instructed the servant to take her leave. She could hardly wait to rush into the arms of the man she so longed for and it seemed that it took an eternity for the servant to leave.

"Oh Damon, I knew you would come!" she whispered as she put her arms around his neck. "I have missed you so very much, and I'm so overjoyed to see you."

"As am I," replied Damon, but instead of holding her he pushed her away. "We have no time for this now. Andrew and I have put together a plan to get you out of here. Are you up to it?"

"Of course, I am," assured Niccoli, "but will the plan put my parents in any more danger than they are already?" Niccoli was concerned of what would happen to her parents if Nero knew they had deliberately hidden her.

"Niccoli, I would never ask you to do anything that would harm your parents. Besides, your father is a man of great influence and I would not want to experience his wrath," Damon replied. "Now, listen closely, this is what you must do. Have your father invite the guard in for a sip of wine and a portion of this bread. It is tainted with poisonous herbs. Yes, I see your look. Don't worry it will not kill him. It is only intended to make him very ill. I will be outside watching and when the bread has done its work, I will come for you. Dress like a servant so you will not be noticed.

I must leave you now before he comes to see what is taking me so long. Do you have any questions?"

Niccoli shook her head. He kissed her on the forehead and was gone before she could say anything else. She watched as he strolled down the street and disappeared around the corner. The thought of escaping gave her mixed emotions. Even though she was excited about the prospect of being free again, she was saddened about leaving her parents. She instinctively knew that it would probably be her final farewell to her mother and quite possibly to her father as well.

"Niccoli, are you ill? You look so pale," Cornelius asked as he entered the room. "The servant said you were in need of me."

"No, Father, I am quite all right," she responded. "I have just seen Damon and he has explained a plan for my escape." She took him aside and proceeded to tell him everything that Damon had told her.

Cornelius was relieved to know that his daughter was going to be taken care of by her fellow Christians. They were at last going to accomplish what he had not been able to do and he was grateful to them. He knew that Damon must have been instrumental in the plan and was so happy that he had introduced him to Niccoli. He mulled over the plan and agreed that it should work, and then focused his attention on the bread. After inspecting it thoroughly, he simply shrugged his shoulders and commented, "It looks like ordinary bread to me."

Niccoli agreed, but suggested they take every precaution to make sure the herbs would not be detected. They decided that the best camouflage would be to pour honey over the servings, and then Cornelius would serve himself the good bread at the same time that he served the guard the tainted bread. It was their hope that when the honey was poured over both, the guard would not notice the difference between the two servings.

Cornelius thought the idea was brilliant and instructed the servant to do as Niccoli suggested. He watched to make sure every detail was carried out and, when he was satisfied with everything, he took the treat outside and invited the guard to join him for a mid-morning snack. He handed the guard the tainted bread and poured his wine. Cornelius smiled at the guard and started a casual conversation.

Niccoli took advantage of the remaining moments to bid her mother goodbye. She was careful of what she said because she did not want to alarm her, and simply stated she would be gone for a short time but assured her that she would return soon.

"Niccoli, please be careful as you travel. There are many robbers that roam the roads," her mother cautioned.

"Please do not worry, Damon is going with me."

It did not take long for the herbs to take effect and the guard was soon bent over from the pain of the stomach cramps that he was experiencing. He cursed Cornelius for his pain and accused him of poisoning either the bread or the wine. Cornelius assured him there was no poison in either the bread or the wine and to substantiate his claim he sipped the wine and ate a portion of the guard's bread. If he fell ill himself it was a small price to pay for his daughter's escape.

Cornelius' actions seemed to calm the soldier and he agreed to the suggestion that he rest in the shade of the trees on the far side of the house. Damon watched the drama unfold from his vantage point. When he saw the servant accompany the soldier to the trees at the opposite side of the house he hastened to retrieve Niccoli.

She was ready when he arrived and after giving her father a final embrace, the two rushed past the empty guard post and down the street; escaping her captor's snare. Damon held Niccoli's hand as they hurried down the street and, even though there were no words spoken between them, Niccoli's heart was full of love and gratitude to Damon for what he had just accomplished for her. It was because of his love, and also the love of her fellow Christians, that she was now free. Freedom was within her grasp as they rounded the corner of the street where the Christians had set up their rendezvous.

"Oh, Damon," Niccoli exclaimed, "it is so wonderful to be outside again! Listen to the birds. Aren't they wonderful? And the sun, it feels so good upon my face. Oh, I am so happy we can be together again. I love you so much! Thank you for freeing me."

Before Damon could respond, a Roman guard seemed to come from nowhere to suddenly cut off their flight. "Is this the Christian woman named Niccoli?" he asked of Damon.

Niccoli shot a quick glance at Damon. He could surely take on this guard and they would soon be on their way.

"Yes, this is she," replied Damon.

Niccoli stared at him, shocked at his reply. Why had he revealed her? She looked from Damon to the soldier in an effort to understand what was happening. "I don't understand," she said in a barely audible voice. She felt herself trembling and the sick feeling in the pit of her stomach told her she had been betrayed. "Damon, why?" she sobbed.

"Niccoli, you are a woman beautiful beyond words, but I could not allow myself to fall in love with you. I am first a Roman soldier," Damon explained, controlling his emotions by not looking at her. "I have to first think of myself and my career. I was commissioned by Nero to bring you and the others to him. You are a fine person and this grieves me, but I have to do what I am ordered to do."

He turned and took a bundle from the soldier and unwrapped it to reveal his Roman centurion armor. He watched Niccoli's reaction as he shed the cloak of a merchant to reveal his centurion tunic. Without hesitation he adorned himself with the highly polished armor and mounted the horse the soldier had brought for him.

"You know, you really are beautiful, and I enjoyed being with you," he said. Shrugging his shoulders he turned his horse around and rode off leaving her to the fate of the soldier standing next to her.

Niccoli was stunned beyond feeling. Many times she had seen him in his armor, but this time it took on an entirely new meaning. She felt herself grow weak as she collapsed to the ground; tears of bitter betrayal streaming down her face. He had only pretended to love her and what they had shared together was as empty as tinkling brass. He was not the Christian man she had thought he was, but rather someone who had a very hard-shelled heart. He was one who thought only of himself and his own selfish wants without a thought of how his actions affected others. He did not comprehend the Christian teachings. Now, because of her faith and trust in Damon, she had also revealed the Christian underground network and sealed the fate of her fellow Christians. She now knew, as Jesus had known, the ultimate hurt: to give totally of oneself, to love without restraints and then see that love tossed aside as though it had no value.

The total realization of the danger she was now facing became evident when the guard jerked her to a standing position and started shackling her feet. She was trapped.

How could she have been so blind? "Oh, Lord, please be with my fellow Christians that I have unknowingly betrayed," she sobbed as she was led away.

CHAPTER 16

Niccoli's body ached from the dampness of the cell in which she was confined. The stench of body waste, left behind by the many prisoners who were held captive before her, was intolerable; the filthy dirt floor a sharp contrast to her father's spotlessly clean marble floors. Looking about for the least filthy place to sit was impossible so she remained standing, that way only her feet would be touching the incrustation of waste. She looked down at the many stains on her dress and wanted to somehow clean them off, but she could not bear the thought of touching the filth so she held her hands out in front of her body in absolute despair. She could fell herself becoming nauseous and fought back the strong urge to vomit.

"My God, what a horrible and despicable place to be!" she cried despairingly. "Why can't everyone love as Jesus did? Why do they feel that they have to inflict such injustices upon others? Is it because their greed and egos have made them think that they were so wonderful and above reproach; all the while thinking that others have no value?"

The long night was unbearable. After standing for so long during the day she became weary and could no longer stand. She finally ignored the filth and huddled in a corner, drawing her knees up to her chest in a hopeless effort to escape the evening draft. She was hungry, depressed and frightened by all of the rats scampering about in the darkness of her cell. Occasionally, a moonbeam would strike their vile eyes and cause them to shine a bright red back at her. She shuddered at the horribly eerie sight and wanted to close her eyes to shut out their image, but she was too terrified that if she did so they would sneak up and attack her. The horrid rodents seemed to come out more at night even though, she thought to herself, they were certainly plentiful enough during the day.

She was having difficulty accepting Damon's rejection and betrayal, and her thoughts again turned back to him. Despite everything she now knew, she wanted it to be as it was before and longed for the warmth of his arms around her again, to hold his hand and walk in the twilight of the evening, to block out the events of the past few days and again be lost in love. But, to her consternation, she had to face the fact that Damon had used her for his personal gain. He had sacrificed her in order to obtain favor from Nero, and his betrayal wounded her deeply.

Now, she had to face up to the fact that because she had trusted Damon her fellow Christians also had been captured, and the thought of them being tortured because of her was almost more than she could endure. The reason that she had worked so hard in the underground network was to provide shelter for the hunted, not to lead them to their deaths. She had wanted to protect them at all costs and was heartsick because there would be no time, or way, for her to make amends. She felt that, even though it had not been her intent, she had betrayed them because of her own selfish desire for Damon.

When she finally dropped off to sleep there was a fervent prayer on her lips for Jesus to help her discover a way to help the others who were confined to similar despicable cells. The cold hard facts foretold the bleak future; the certainty that their lives would end in the arena with the lions feeding on them while the Roman people watched and laughed at their slaughter.

She was awakened the next morning by something brushing against her leg. Sleepily, she moved the folds of her dress to reveal a fat rat crawling inside her skirt. With a shriek she instantly was on her feet, jumping up and down until the terrified rodent fell to the ground. With a shrill squeak the rat ran to the other side of the room to escape Niccoli's vengeance and quickly squeezed under the heavy door of the cell. She shuddered and swore that she would never again allow herself to fall asleep and give the nasty pests an opportunity to get that close again.

She looked around for a place to sit that was somewhat cleaner than the rest of the cell and thought back to what Jesus had taught. He always said that everyone was God's creation and all were created equal in God's eyes. That being so, it was evident to Niccoli that no one should treat another with indignities such as those she now was experiencing.

It was Damon who had ordered the Roman soldiers to separate Niccoli from the others because of her great influence over them. He did not want her to give them encouragement or hope. They had done as he wished and put her in a cell by herself. In sharp contrast, however, her fellow Christians were crammed into small cells that allowed them only standing room. She could not see them, but she could hear them pleading for water and food. Men were swearing their vengeance and the sound of crying children could be heard in the background. She felt the strong desire to comfort and console them, but how could she when she was so isolated from them?

The air was thick with despair, and Niccoli felt so helpless. Then, as though Jesus had whispered in her ear, a thought occurred to her. She could do as David had done in the past and sing the songs of encouragement, dedication, love, and of joy and comfort. It did not matter if they could not see her because they could hear her. Hearing would be enough for now. She said a prayer of thanksgiving to Jesus for giving her the insight on how to give her friends the encouragement she knew they needed.

Andrew was not aware of the fact that Niccoli was located three cells up from him. He had no way of knowing if she had escaped or had been killed. He only knew that she wasn't in his cell with the others. He could only deduce that she had already been killed when Damon had arrived at their rendezvous dressed in his centurion garb. Instead of bringing Niccoli as had been planned, he was leading Roman soldiers. It readily became obvious to Andrew and the others that they had been betrayed.

Andrew remembered the smirk on Damon's face as he looked down from his horse and mockingly said. 'I want to thank you for giving me this opportunity to gain favor with Nero. I am deeply grateful to you.' He had laughed loudly as he kicked Andrew with such force that it sent him sprawling to the ground.

'Where is Niccoli?' Andrew had demanded as he looked up at his betrayer.

'You need not worry, she has already been taken care of,' was Damon's response as he turned his horse around and began to circle the captives. 'Round up these Christians and be quick about it,' he yelled at the soldiers. 'Nero does not want to wait any longer. He is anxious to see them put in cells where they rightfully belong and where he will have easy access to use them for his enjoyment.' Andrew remembered watching him as he rode around spouting out orders. Yes, beyond question, Damon had deceived him and, worse yet, his pretense had also betrayed Niccoli. Lust for power had obviously been his motivation.

'Move!' Andrew remembered the order had resounded. 'Stick your leg out so that I might tie this rope around your ankle!' the soldier had ordered. Soon the Christians were being herded down the street like a flock of sheep. They were filled with terror and the realization that they were now at the mercy of their accusers.

Andrew was quiet as he stood in his odious cell. His thoughts were of Niccoli and he could only imagine the pain that she must have felt when she realized the man she loved had betrayed her. He was thinking of what he would do to Damon, if he would ever have the opportunity to get his hands on him, when out of the quiet of the night he heard singing. Tears whelmed in his eyes when he recognized the voice of Niccoli singing songs of hope and encouragement to her fellow prisoners.

Her singing shot like a bolt of lightning through the cells and soon the prisoners were whispering to one another, "It is Niccoli, she is alive! She is here with us! Glory be to the Father!" It reassured them to know that she was alive and near. Joining hands with the one standing near, they fell silent and listened to her song:

There are times when the load gets heavy,
When we are not free, but have to stay.
There are times when all seems against us,
And sleep seems so far away.

However, never lose hope, and never lose faith,
The two hand in hand reign.
Only when these are gone is there darkness,
But, even then the light shall reign again.

So rejoice, my fellow prisoners, rejoice!
Their battle will never be won.
They can destroy our earthly bodies,
But our souls shall forever remain on.

Rejoice! I say to you, rejoice!
Our reward is now close at hand.
We shall see Jesus in all of His glory,
And dwell together with God's glorious band.

The guards who were standing on the outside of the walls listened as Niccoli sang and could sense the comfort that she was giving to the other prisoners. They could feel the power of the moment as the prisoners quieted. Damon had been right; she did have great influence over them. It troubled one guard more than the others and he voiced his concern. "We must make her stop," he said. "We cannot take the chance that she will get the others riled into a rebellion."

"What does it matter?" the second guard responded. "They will not live long enough to organize."

As they spoke, the sound of the roaring lions could be heard in the background. They purposely had not been fed in preparation for the event that was about to take place, and they were beginning to get restless and nasty from the hunger they felt.

Rumor had it that the day of their execution would be on the Sabbath, only two days away. Nero seemed to find humor in the fact that he was sending Christians to their death on the day they had set aside to worship their Lord. He would not, however, be sending all of them to their death. Some he would hold back so that they might chase the lions back into their dens when the entertainment was over. Others would gather up the remains of whatever was left of their fellow Christians and family members after the lions had finished feeding on them. Their fate would come at a later date.

"Nero has to be the most inhuman, sadistic person that has ever lived," Niccoli angrily said to herself. She understood what was happening at nightfall when the guards chose the fatter of the prisoners and led them away. She had heard how Christians were being tied to stakes and covered with oil and olive pits and, while still alive, set afire to be used as human torches. Their burning bodies would light up the beautifully manicured palace gardens so that Nero could see to drive his chariot recklessly down the pathways. It was said that his face shone with excitement when he raced at top speed, laughing uproariously at the fate of the Christians. "Where is your God now?" he would jeer as he flew by them.

Niccoli knew that some of the Christians were asking the same question. "Why has our God forsaken us?' Others did not think that He had forsaken them, but instead affirmed, "It is God's will that we are being persecuted," although they did not understand why it must be so. Everyone was extremely bitter about being betrayed by Damon and their hearts were full of revenge.

Niccoli understood what her fellow Christians were going through, she above all felt the sting of betrayal. She also remembered similar emotions many years prior and reflected back to what had made her change those feelings of hate and revenge after that unforgettable night in the alley. It had been Jesus. She remembered how He had taught her to love instead of hate, and to release the hurts and negative feelings that were standing in the way of her happiness. He had told her she must forgive her transgressors and put aside what they had done to her so that she could begin to love again without restraint. By releasing the past, He explained, she would become as a child again which would enable her to have a fresh start. Niccoli did as Jesus asked, and over the years she had learned to pray in this manner: 'Dear Father in heaven, I no longer give this hurt any power over my life. I lay the hurt at your feet and will not dwell on it any longer. It is now in the past. Through your guidance and help, dear Jesus, teach me to love and forgive. I ask this in your precious name...Amen.'

Somehow she must again remind the others of that message of love. She had to make them understand that the issue was not what the Romans were doing to them, but rather how they themselves reacted to the Roman injustices. There was only one way that the Romans could take away their dignity, if they themselves allowed it to happen. They had to remember that the Roman heathens could only kill their earthly bodies; they did not have the power to destroy their Christian souls. So, that evening Niccoli sang:

> Jesus taught us to love all people,
> To forgive those who have wronged us,
> And love them as our own.
>
> Today, people will be watching,
> Their frenzy governed by mob rule,
> As God's love is lost among them,
>
> So chose your actions carefully,
> For you are the living examples,
> That allows God's love to shine through.

After her songs the prisoners seemed to calm down, but it was not long before the guards returned and Niccoli could hear them take away more prisoners. She assumed that Nero must be racing his chariots; again using her fellow Christians as human torches to light the paths as he recklessly raced around the palace gardens. Anger rose in Niccoli and she fell to her knees in prayer.

"Father in heaven," she prayed, "Master of forgiveness, help me to overcome this extreme anger. I do not want it to consume me. Help me to forgive my enemies for what they are doing and to understand why they are doing such a thing. Be with those who have been taken to Nero's gardens. Spare their lives if possible, and if not, may their deaths be painless.

I ask this in the precious name of Jesus. Amen."

It was several hours after the Christians had been led away that Niccoli was aroused by the sound of the guards talking excitedly outside. She quietly moved towards the door to better hear what they were saying.

"I have never seen anything like it!" one guard exclaimed. "The Christians were singing all the way as we escorted them to the palace last night."

"So, what is so exciting about that?" asked the other.

"Wait, let me finish. We tied them to the stakes in the garden and they never stopped singing, even long after we put the torch to them. I could not believe my ears or my eyes! I have never seen anything like it before in my life. What kind of God do they believe in that can bestow such bravery? Perhaps we should look into it, for I too would like to be so brave."

"You had best watch what you say," replied the other, "or you will be walking alongside of them the next time they go to the gardens."

Niccoli listened and praised the Lord. He had heard her intercessory prayer and had filled the dying Christians with the Holy Spirit to the point of overcoming their pain. "Thank you, sweet Jesus," Niccoli whispered. "Thank you."

The night was quiet except for the roars of the restless lions. Hunger definitely was not helping their dispositions. The roars grew louder and the prisoners stood motionless in their cells, listening to the beasts. They knew that their fates had been sealed and that there was no way of escaping the inevitable.

"Even though I walk through the valley of the shadow of death, I will fear no evil;" Niccoli chanted, "for thou art with me. Surely goodness and mercy shall follow me all the days of my life and I will dwell in the house of the Lord forever.

It was as though the scripture had been written explicitly for them. Yes, they were walking through the 'Valley of the Shadow of Death' at this very moment, but they were at peace with God.

"He has promised us there is life after our physical death. Do you remember?" questioned Andrew as he picked up where Niccoli had stopped. "He has promised us that death is only a crossing over to a life that will be so glorious; the pain and disappointment will be gone. Rejoice! He has not deserted us, nor will He ever desert us. He never caused the Romans to do what they are doing to us. They themselves decided to persecute us. It's not God's will, but theirs. Take heart, and sing together the songs that we have sung together many times before in our services," he encouraged.

Slowly, one by one, they joined Andrew and Niccoli in song. Soon the spirit of the Lord fell heavy upon them, and they felt a closeness and love for each other that they had never felt before. They bonded together in a way that has been known to only a select few.

They used the remaining hours to say their goodbyes and reminisce about things they had previously shared together. All too soon the dawn of early morning stole into their cells and it was the morning of the Sabbath, the designated day of their deaths. Andrew solemnly started the last formal worship in which they would participate.

The guards stood outside their cells and listened while they read the scriptures and sang. They were beginning to take an interest in these people, their belief in their God and why they were so willing to give their lives for Him.

Time was drawing to a close, a fact that Niccoli did not want to acknowledge, so she focused on her friends' singing. Suddenly she heard the clink of the lock on the door and she knew it was time for them to be ushered down the corridor and into the arena. "Sweet Jesus, be with me in this final hour. May I be a witness for You," she prayed quietly.

She breathlessly waited and watched as the guard opened the door but, to her surprise, instead of commanding her to come out he stepped inside and closed the door. Niccoli, stunned by his actions, suspiciously watched him as he approached. What did he want? She stood frozen and waited for his next move. When he drew closer she could see him more clearly and suddenly recognized him. She pressed her hand against her mouth to suppress the scream that was springing up in her throat. Realizing how unprotected she was, and knowing there was no escape available, all the color drained from her face.

Again she looked at him in the hope that she was mistaken. No, she would remember that face always even though he was years older. All the old feelings of that terrifying night in the alley overwhelmed her, and she tearfully waited to see what he was going to do.

"I see you recognize me," Marcos said in a quiet voice. He was obviously very nervous and fidgeted with the bracelet on his arm before he continued. "Please do not be afraid of me. I mean you no harm." His voice quivered as he spoke. "This is not easy for me. I have come to ask your forgiveness. You have haunted me ever since that horrible night in the alley, and I have not had one drop of strong wine since. I heard the story of how Jesus healed you and I was extremely thankful. However, I still had to come to you and ask your forgiveness. Words cannot explain the remorse that I feel. Can you ever forgive me for what I did to you?" He fell to his knees at Niccoli's feet, taking no notice of the stench and filth in the cell. His only concern was to obtain her forgiveness.

Niccoli looked down at him and put her hands on his shoulders. "I forgave you years ago," she stated as she motioned for him to rise. "Jesus taught me to forgive those who have wronged me. He explained that if I did not forgive you and the others I would allow hatred to build up inside of me, which would result in me being a very unhappy and bitter person. I asked for His help to forgive you and He gave it to me. All the feelings of hate disappeared and I was able to again love and trust others."

"You see, Marcos, to forgive you was vital for my own well-being and peace. Now, you have come to me seeking the same peace by asking for my forgiveness. Through the understanding of forgiveness we are both better people, you for feeling remorse and wanting forgiveness, and me for laying aside my feelings of hate and revenge to forgive you. Walk away from here today with the assurance that God will forgive you as well. Lay aside your guilt, ask for and accept God's forgiveness. Leave with a new outlook on life and pass this forgiveness on to others. Thank God for giving us Jesus who was a living example of love and forgiveness. His life was one that you can pattern your life after. Know that the Lord loves you. Go in peace. May God richly bless you."

Marcos looked at her and felt peace throughout his body. True, he had wanted her forgiveness, but he could not imagine how she would ever be able to forgive such a horrible act. "Thank you," he managed to mumble.

Marcos left the cell knowing that he had just been with the most gracious and noble lady he had ever known. When he closed the door behind him he felt as though a great weight had been lifted from his shoulders and wished there was something he could do for her. However, he had to face the fact that circumstances were far beyond his control.

CHAPTER 17

"Oh, Mighty One," praised Damon. "Ruler of the one great Nation, may I humbly partition a favor of you."

"Speak, what is it? You have earned the right," replied Nero, not really caring if Damon responded. He took a drink of his wine and motioned to his servant to replenish the now empty goblet.

"Please, if I may, I would ask you to spare the life of a Christian named Niccoli," pleaded Damon.

"Niccoli. That name sounds familiar," Nero responded as he tapped his fore-finger on his chin while he tried to recall the name.

"Yes, Grand One, she is the daughter of Senator Cornelius Cademus," Damon interjected.

"Ah, yes. What does she have to do with you?" Nero asked.

"She is one of the Christians who will be going into the arena today."

"Why then, by all the gods in the heavens, do you want me to spare her life? You know I hate all Christians and so you should!" Nero exclaimed.

"Yes, I know, but if you allow me but a short time with her

I know I can convince her to give up this Jesus. She is beautiful and would make a wonderful mother of my children. She loves me, or did, and I would like to claim her as my own if you so deemed," replied Damon.

"Your manliness overshadows you reason," Nero huffed, sneering at the man standing before him. He did not understand such love.

"Perhaps so, your exalted one."

"If you can convince her to give up her God, then she is all yours, but I do hope you are not disappointed. Why don't you let me find someone who would be much better suited to you? There are many who would lay down their life for you," stated Nero. Laughing at the proposal he continued, "How apropos! Lay down their life."

"I am quite sure you can find many who would do as you say. Perhaps even become my wife, but this one is special!" Damon assured his ruler.

"Do what you must; you have earned a favor. Go!" Nero said with a flip of his hand. "Make yourself happy, although I do not understand your desires."

Damon saluted, backed out of the room and hurried to the imprisonment. As he approached the cells the stench became intolerable and he covered his nose to filter out the smell. He motioned for the jailer to unlock the cell where Niccoli was imprisoned. 'What a deplorable place for such a lovely creature as Niccoli', he thought.

When Damon entered the cell he stood in disbelief. Niccoli was in the far corner of the cell and when she turned to see who had entered, he hardly recognized her. The two days had already taken a toll on her beauty and he was totally appalled by her appearance. He was about to turn away when she asked, "Damon, why are you here?" Her voice showed little emotion.

Damon hesitated, thinking over his decision before he replied. "I have come to take you away from this."

"And just how do you intend to do that?"

"I have asked Nero to spare your life," explained Damon.

"And why should you do such a thing?"

"Because I love you," he replied.

"Just like that? You love me and I am free?"

"Well, no, Nero would never approve of that. I had to tell him that you would renounce Jesus," Damon responded.

"I can not do that," responded Niccoli.

"But you must! I can not save you unless you do," Damon pleaded.

"I can not," Niccoli repeated firmly.

"Do you know what you are saying?" Damon's anger was beginning to flare.

"I know what I am saying," Niccoli acknowledged.

"Then you love a dead man more than you love me?" Damon's face was turning red. The veins in his neck were beginning to protrude. How could she turn him down?

"I love Him differently than I loved you," explained Niccoli.

"Oh, now it is loved, not love."

"I love you as a person."

"But not as a lover, is that it?"

"Yes, I no longer love you as a lover."

"Niccoli, you are not thinking clearly. I know that you love me, you are just angry with me right now. Don't you realize that if you turn me down I will not be able to help you? Your fate will be the lions."

"If it is meant to be."

"You are crazy!" Damon roared as he stormed out of the cell, the door clanking loudly behind him.

Niccoli flinched at the sound. Just a few simple words and she could be free. All she had to do was to call after him and her life would be spared. Perhaps she was crazy. Damon certainly believed it.

"What is the matter, Damon?" jeered a guard. "She chose

Jesus over you? A dead man! Perhaps you were not man enough for her?"

Damon reeled about and drew his sword. He was about to strike the guard when another soldier grabbed his arm, "It is not worth it, Damon. Do not jeopardize your career."

The first guard had his hand on his sword, his eyes flashing with the prospect of a fight. "Come ahead, fight me," he challenged.

Damon hesitated and then rammed his sword back into its sheath. He took a few steps towards the jeering guard and said in a threatening voice, "Stay clear of me. You will not be so lucky next time. I will not forget this encounter. There will come a time that you will be at my mercy!" He turned to leave just as Master Gladiator brushed past him. His bright red mantel rippled in the wind as he hurried towards the guards in his haste to execute Nero's desires.

"Damon," he mumbled in passing recognition and then focused on the guards. "Guards," he boomed, "gather five of the finest of these so called Christian men, and bring them to me!"

"As you order, so it will be," replied one of the guards as they all scampered to examine the men held captive in the cells. They carefully scanned each one and finally made the selection with five of the most muscular men, Andrew among them.

"Hurry, do not keep Master Gladiator waiting," the guard ordered as he pushed them ahead. "You have been honored."

Soon all were lined up in front of the Gladiator for him to inspect. He viewed them with disgust, but carefully checked their muscle tone and build.

"You have done a good job, my fellow comrades," he said to the guards in congratulations and then turned to the prisoners; with an air of importance he began his canned speech. "Now, listen to what I have to say! Nero has given me the authority to mold you into Gladiators!" he boasted as he strutted in front of them. "You will live in luxury while you bout, and will be allowed to live for as long as you continue to win your bouts. Even though I am sure you will not agree with me, today is especially a good day because you will be performing before Nero! Follow me and hurry along, the crowd is impatiently waiting."

"We do not care to give pleasure to Nero." Andrew scoffed.

"Ah, someone has spirit here. But it matters not what you desire to do or not to do. I am sure that when you are confronted with the realization of life or death, you will fight to stay alive and forget all about pleasing Nero," Master Gladiator commented. "A lesson we all had to learn."

"What if we refuse?" Andrew asked.

"No matter. You will be returned to your cell and will face the lions at a later time. So you see, you really have no choice in the matter," he said. He stepped closer and surveyed Andrew before continuing, "I like your looks! You will be the first Gladiator."

"You can not force me to kill my opponent," Andrew said with determination.

"You will, or be killed yourself," the Gladiator added nonchalantly.

The men were led to a room just off the arena and handed clean clothes that were designed especially for the gladiator bout. They quietly washed away the filth and dressed. Even though they felt awkward in the new attire, it felt good to be clean again.

Andrew could hear the crowd demanding action. They had worked themselves into frenzy and were anxious for the first bout. Master Gladiator chained the men together and led them to the arena. When they entered, the sound of the people cheering and applauding was deafening. "Fight! Fight! Fight!" they chanted.

Master Gladiator bowed in response to their request. He

waved his arm toward the Christian men as if to say: 'They are here and ready to do as you command,' and then he held up his arms in a gesture for them to quiet down.

"These are Christian men who are awaiting their persecution," he yelled out to them and, keeping his hand up in recognition of their presence, he turned full circle to acknowledge everyone in the stadium. "I have hand picked them to be Gladiators. Do you want to see what kind of fight they have left in themselves?"

"Yes!" the crowd roared.

"Alright then, let the bout begin!" He smiled as he took the key from his belt to unlock Andrew's chains. "My brave one," he mocked, "are you ready?"

Andrew just looked at him and did not give him the satisfaction of an answer.

"Suit yourself. I do not worry about my back, but you should watch yours," he laughed, feeling smug with his humor.

Just then the door opened on the other side of the arena and a giant of a man emerged. Andrew stared at him in disbelief. He carried with him a sword, shield and a large rock that was wrapped with strips of leather with a long strap attached. He had a scar on the right cheek and his arm was bandaged. Andrew watched him as he defiantly walked into the center of the arena and motioned for him to join him.

Andrew swallowed hard and looked at his fellow Christians. Their eyes were round with terror as they watched, fearful for Andrew. He looked back at the man waiting for him, and barely noticed the feel of the cold steel of a sword being thrust into his hand by Master Gladiator. "Here take this shield. You will need it," he said as he pushed Andrew forward.

Without looking back, Andrew entered the arena. The crowd roared with delight when they saw him and then hushed as they waited in anticipation of a good fight. His opponent laughed at him from across the arena. With a loud yell, he came running towards him whirling the leather strap in a circle above his head, took aimed and hurled the rock towards Andrew who quickly ducked and stepped aside. The crowd cheered the maneuver. Again he lunged at Andrew and again he missed the mark.

"Boo!" roared the crowd. They wanted to see blood spill from their bodies.

"Coward, fight me!" yelled the giant.

Andrew watched as his opponent started to circle him. His heart was racing and he felt himself trembling, partly from fear and partly from the adrenalin racing through his veins.

"Ha, you are frightened. I see you trembling," the giant snarled. He circled one more time and then jumped at Andrew, cutting Andrew's arm with his sword as he passed him.

Andrew looked down and saw the blood running down his arm and onto the top of his hand. He shook his head to clear his mind. He could not allow anything to break his concentration. Again he looked at his opponent and made a wide circle, but this time he would be the one to take control.

"Yes, come to me," his opponent taunted.

Andrew bent his body slightly into a crouched position and swayed back and forth, ready to move in either direction when his opponent came after him. He did not have long to wait. When the huge one thought he had the advantage again he lunged at Andrew and swirled the leather strapped rock over his head. Andrew was ready for him and he waited until the last second before he ducked and sidestepped him. He then sank his sword into the giant's wrist causing the rock to fling uncontrollably from his hand.

The giant drew back; surprised that Andrew had become so aggressive. He sneered, ignoring the cut, and circled Andrew again. He, as well as Andrew, had tuned the crowd out and were aware of nothing but each other. There was no doubt that the combat had escalated and that Andrew was seriously fighting for his life.

With a loud war cry the giant came at him again. Andrew blocked his thrust, and again his sword hit its mark and sank into the giant's shoulder. He grabbed at his wounded shoulder and cursed Andrew loudly.

"Stop," Andrew pleaded, "I do not want to kill you."

"But I want to kill you! I want your head," the big man snarled.

Both men were bleeding profusely now and each was feeling the effects of the lost blood. "You are mine!" growled the giant and raised his sword over his head with the intent of sinking it into Andrew's skull. Andrew dodged the move and with a flying leap he kicked the giant in the upper chest and knocked him to the ground, causing his sword to fly out of his hand. The giant warrior lay stunned for a moment; he looked for his sword and realized that it was too far for him to retrieve. He made an effort to get up but Andrew hit him with his forearm and knocked him back to the ground and quickly stepped on his chest; pressing his sword against his throat.

The crowd was at their peak of excitement. "Kill him!" they yelled. "Slash his throat!"

"I will not kill this man!" Andrew yelled. He looked down at the man waiting for his death.

"Kill him! Kill him!" screamed the crowd.

Andrew looked down at his opponent. "If I let you up will you go in peace?"

"Yes, I am at your mercy," was the reply.

Andrew yelled to the crowd, "I wish not to kill this man! He has done me no wrong. I therefore release him so that he can fight for you again."

"Boo!" the crowd yelled. They were on their feet by now and shaking their fists at Andrew. They wanted satisfaction.

"Do as you are told! Kill him! Kill him!" yelled Master

Gladiator.

"Not today," Andrew said and released his foe.

The crowd was in a frenzy by now, anxious to continue with the brutality, and the more brutal, the better. They were thirsty for blood and wanted more than what Andrew was willing to give them. "Bring out the lions! Bring out the lions!" they chanted in a deafening roar. "Lions, lions, bring out the lions!"

The prisoners could hear the crowd yelling to bring out the lions and wondered what had been the outcome of the bout. Which one of their group had died at the end of a sword? With the bout over the dreaded time had now arrived! It did not take the guards long to arrive at their cells and herd them into the corridor and for the first time Niccoli was able to see her captured friends. She embraced each one that she could reach, and begged for their forgiveness as they walked down the long corridor.

"Remember, Niccoli, Jesus was also betrayed, tortured and killed." said one of the faithful. "You are not to blame for this, it is the Romans that have done this to us."

"Yes," replied Niccoli, "they do not comprehend who we are, or what they are doing to us. They think only of their own enjoyment; crude and harsh as it may be."

"Shut your mouths!" yelled a guard and he started shoving them forward.

Niccoli smiled at her comrades. "Stand tall!" she encouraged. "Remember that Jesus forgave those who wronged him, just as we must also forgive the Romans. God be with you, my fellow Christians." She turned, straightened herself to her full height and walked to the front of the prisoners. "Jesus, Jesus, Jesus," she chanted as she led them toward the arena.

When they drew close to the cage like door, Niccoli saw two gladiators standing next to the gate. A closer look revealed one to be Andrew. "Andrew!" she cried.

"Yes, I am still here, they cannot kill me so easily," he

joked as he rushed towards her.

"You are bleeding!"

"I am fine, do not fuss over me! They forced me into a bout and I won, but I spared the man's life. The crowd was quite angry with me when they could not force me to kill for them. Master Gladiator was furious and, even though I won, he condemned me to death by making me go with the rest of you to face the lions. He does not know it, but he did me a favor when he enabled me to walk beside you into the arena." Andrew took her hand as he spoke.

"Oh, Andrew," whispered Niccoli. "You have been a true and devoted friend. I was so foolish to have believed in Damon. Can you ever forgive me?"

"It does not matter. I, nor any of the others, find blame with you. We all know that you have always looked out for our best interests," Andrew confirmed. He put his arms around her in an effort to comfort her and she laid her head on his shoulders and cried. How could they forgive her so readily?

Suddenly, the guards interrupted them by slapping something on their shoulders. Niccoli looked down to find the skin of a freshly slain animal thrown over her shoulder. She screamed and threw it to the ground.

The guard laughed at her response and replied, "It matters not if you take it off for the scent of its blood is still on you and that is enough to attract the lions.

Niccoli looked at Andrew, his tunic also was stained with the animal's blood. Their eyes met, and each reflected the hopelessness that they felt for the situation.

"Farewell my friend," he said to her as they walked hand in hand across the threshold and into the arena, "God be with you and God willing it be over quickly."

"Yes, and God be with you," whispered Niccoli.

The door slammed behind the Christians with such a loud clang that they jumped at the sound. They looked around the arena and noticed that the dirt floor was soaked with the blood of others that had died previously. The stonewall that encircled the arena was built much higher than their heads and they instantly knew that they were trapped. There was no possible escape!

Niccoli looked at the opposite end of the arena and saw the huge lions pacing back and forth behind the bars of their cages. She lifted her gaze to the crowd seated high above her in anticipation of a great spectacle, and sensed how eager they were to see what kind of entertainment she and the others would provide for them.

In the middle deck she saw a large black canopy with gold tassels hanging at each corner and knew that it had to be a place of distinction. Upon closer observation she saw Nero sitting proud and pompous under the canopy, his purple robe draped across his legs and his chin cupped in his hand while resting his elbow upon his knee. Beside him was a centurion dressed in full uniform and she gasped when she realized that it was Damon. All of the hurt and anger that she had prayed so hard to erase from her heart flooded over her again. It hurt deeply to see him sitting on his velvet draped perch. She wondered if he felt proud of the accomplishments that had earned him this place of honor.

Damon looked down at her and for a split second their eyes locked upon each other. He could see by her expression all the hurt, frustration and fear that she was feeling because of his betrayal. Her slender body appeared so fragile compared to the huge bodies of the lions pacing in the background.

Guilt forced him to turn his face away from her and immediately he realized that Nero had been observing him with keen interest. He quickly regained his composure and forced a smile in Nero's direction to confirm he was enjoying the spectator sport.

The quiet was deafening as everyone waited for Nero's signal to begin the game. One of his concubines brought him wine in his golden goblet, and he lifted the goblet towards the Christians to toast them in mockery. Damon noticed the excitement that danced in Nero's eyes, and when his goblet was filled, he lifted it in acknowledgment of his commanding officer and then, with a nod of his head and a slight bow, he followed Nero's lead and also toasted the Christians.

Feeling smug in the power that he had over life and death, Nero rose and raised his hands over his head. He made sure that all eyes were upon him. When he was confident that he had their attention he hesitated and then with a smirk on his face, he turned his thumbs down. With that one simple gesture the half starved lions were released on the defenseless Christians and the crowd went crazy with anticipation.

Niccoli stood her ground as others around her ran in vain attempts to hide or find a weapon to defend themselves. With determination she continued to walk forward into the face of death still chanting, "Jesus, Jesus, Jesus," with every step that she took.

She heard the piercing screams of the men and women around her as the hungry lions pounced upon their prey. She turned her head in time to see a lion springing towards her, but she did not have time to avoid his attack. His total body was suspended in mid-air when she felt his huge claws dig deep into her shoulders. The force of the impact caused her to fall back, hitting her head on a large rock that was half hidden in the dirt of the arena floor. Everything went black, and the horror of the event was over for Niccoli.

Damon watched as the lion lay down to feed upon Niccoli's body, its paws placed on each side of her still form. It was almost too much to witness, but he forced himself to gain his composure and pushed aside his feelings of guilt by justifying his actions as that of a soldier fulfilling the duties that were expected of him.

The crowd went wild over the spectacle before them and few gave any thought for the tragic victims, viewing them only as pawns in a magnificent game. There were, however, some who were astonished at the bravery that Niccoli and the others had displayed. They wondered in their hearts if they could have found the courage to walk forward into the face of certain death as they had done. The sight would leave an impact on them for the rest of lives, and a spark of interest in this Christian God was beginning to tug at their hearts.

Marcos, being a recipient of that Christian love, watched the desecration and for the first time in his life felt the need to fervently pray to Niccoli's God.

CHAPTER 18

Marcos remained seated long after the other spectators had left the coliseum. He shook his head and buried his face in his hands in an effort to blot out the screams of the slain that were still echoing in his mind, but he could not. Their cries still haunted him, and he knew that he could no longer be an impartial spectator. The day had opened his eyes to the insensitivity of himself and the Roman people, and he now realized that the horrid slaughter of innocent people for Nero's sense of pleasure was inexcusable. Niccoli and the other Christian faces were no longer anonymous game players with meaningless existences. They were people who, like himself, thirsted for life.

He looked down at the lions feeding upon their prey and wanted desperately to call an end to all the terror and brutality that was escalating in Rome; but he was only one man, how could he make a difference? How could he stand up against an emperor like Nero? Were there other Romans, not necessarily Christians, who felt as he did?

He rose to leave, and for the first time realized he was not alone. Standing partially hidden by one of the columns was a Roman Senator. Was he spying on him? His heart pounded in his ears as he thought of the possibility of being the next victim. He waited quietly for the Senator to come forward but he remained rigidity fixed. He appeared to be leaning against the column for support and upon closer observation Marcos recognized Senator Cademus. Had he been standing there all along? Did he witness the slaughter of his daughter?

He could not imagine the pain that Cornelius must be feeling after witnessing his only child die; one who was now lying on the arena floor between the paws of a lion. He watched as the grieving man straightened himself and turn to face him. He did not know what he should do or say. Had Niccoli told her father about that night so long ago? Would Cornelius lash out at him? He wanted to escape, but for some reason his feet would not move.

"Did you know my daughter?" asked Cornelius. "Did you know of her beauty and charm?"

"Yes, I knew your daughter. She was the most loving and compassionate person I have ever known," responded Marcos.

"Are you one of the Christians?"

"No, I am not."

"What was your contact with her?"

"She forgave me for something I had done many years ago."

"Yes, she was like that," replied Cornelius.

"Is there anything I can do for you, sir?"

"I am sorry, you must forgive me," apologized Cornelius. "Since it has become common knowledge that I am the father of a Christian, it has been increasingly difficult to recognize friend from foe. Do you truly mean it when you say you want to help me?"

"Yes, I am your humble servant," replied Marcos.

"Very well, I wish for you to retrieve Niccoli's remains and bring her to me so that I might give her a proper burial. In doing so, you do realize what implications that might have?"

Marcos did not respond immediately, but simply stared back at Cornelius. He turned and looked at the lions and was not at all certain he could fulfill such a request. They did seem to be content enough now that their stomachs were full, and each had found their own place to settle down and lick their paws. They looked like the picture of perfect contentment.

"It is done," he finally said as he turned back to face Cornelius. "Take your chariot to the alcove down the street and I will meet you there."

"The God's blessings upon you," replied Cornelius. "I will not forget this."

Marcos watched the grieving man until he was out of sight and wondered how he could fulfill such a request. Cautiously he descended the steps that led to the corridor beneath the arena floor. The stench of death that hovered over him was stifling as he made his way down the dark passageway. He had been in many battles and smelled death before, but this was different. The dirt floor of the arena not only smelled of the new blood today, but also of the stale blood that it had soaked up from the many who had gone before. Even though he was a warrior, it turned his stomach because it was so unjust. These people were not warriors, not even criminals; simply law abiding citizens.

He stopped for a moment to let his eyes adjust to the darkness, and then started toward the torches that were lit at the end of the corridor. As he drew nearer he could see that the corridor opened into a small room, and when he stepped over the threshold he saw the remaining Christians huddled together in total shock over the ordeal they had just witnessed. One woman had removed herself from reality and was crouched into a tight fetal position with her eyes closed. Another was crying softly as she rocked back and forth. A man paced as he wrung his hands in despair, not knowing what to do to stop the brutality. They had just lost their leaders and many of them had lost their entire families. Gathering their remains would be extremely difficult, if not impossible, for them.

Marcos' heart went out to them and he was trying to find the words to comfort them when suddenly someone slapped him on the back. He reeled around ready to fight but dropped his guard when he recognized two of his fellow soldiers. "What are you trying to do? Frighten ten years off my life?" Marcos exclaimed as he pretended to box with his comrades.

They all laughed and a ray of hope started to dawn for Marcos. He knew that it would take little coaxing to convince these particular men to take a few hours off and leave him in charge of the now docile Christians. If they would go along with the offer he was about to present to them he would have the time and opportunity needed to retrieve Niccoli.

"Been with any wild women lately?" Marcos asked in a jovial voice.

The two laughed heartily and drew him into a huddle to swap stories. Marcos listened politely as they told of their conquests, and then whispered in their ears as though he had the greatest secret of all. They listened intently and were soon elbowing each other in confirmation of how great his experience was, and stated they would certainly love to meet this woman of contortions.

"Well, if you are truly interested, perhaps you could hurry over there now," encouraged Marcos. "These Christians have no fight left in them. Just look at them; it will be no problem at all to watch over them. Go! Have fun! I'll see you in a couple of hours." By the time Marcos had finished speaking he had literally pushed them out the door.

Convinced that Marcos was a great friend with a wonderful idea, the two gave an emphatic holler and were soon down the street in quest of more enjoyable ways to spend the afternoon.

Marcos watched the two men until they were out of sight,

and then turned back to the Christians. He wondered if they would be capable of understanding his intention to recover Niccoli's body. However, to his delight, he explained his plan and they seemed to rally. It gave them something to hold on to, a reason to continue.

They rose and, together as a unit, started rounding up the now lazy lions in much the same way a dog would gather sheep. Soon all the lions were back in their cages to wait yet another slaughter.

Niccoli's body was retrieved and what was left of her was placed at the feet of Marcos; a Roman soldier so unlike the other soldiers that they had encountered since the time of their capture. He looked down at the almost unrecognizable body before him and the sight of it was more than he could handle. He suddenly felt extremely ill, and, dropping the burial cloth that he had clutched in his hand, ran for the outside door. All that he could think about was to get fresh air into his lungs. Once outside he leaned against the wall and took deep breaths until the nausea subsided.

"Why?" he cried in frustration as he hit his fists against the coliseum wall in anger. Why was this horrible injustice happening? What had these people done to deserve such punishment? Especially Niccoli who had earned his respect and love.

Fighting to regain his composure he re-entered the coliseum. He was relieved to see that the followers had already taken the burial cloth and had bound the body. He looked at them and tried to speak, but he could not find the words. He nodded his head in gratitude. Each knew there was nothing that could be said to erase the pain and instead, shared the mutual understanding of the sorrow that was felt by all.

Silently Marcos picked up the corpse and hid it only moments before his fun loving comrades returned. "Marcos, you are the best," one congratulated, "and you have also done our jobs for us. A man for all men I would say!"

Marcos slapped each of his comrades on their back, made his excuse to leave and headed for the fresh air again; anxious to meet Cornelius at their designated rendezvous.

Meanwhile, Cornelius parked his chariot near the coliseum in the deserted alcove that had been decided upon earlier. He made sure that he was well hidden from the view of anyone who might pass along the street. Alone in the quiet, all the events of the day started to overwhelm him, and he felt so helpless knowing there was nothing he could have done to prevent the horrible slaughter of his only child. The fact that he was a member of the senate had little value at the time he needed it most. Instead, he had lost his daughter and was now in fear of losing his life.

He was so consumed by grief and anger that he did not notice the silhouette of a man entering the alcove and taking the reins of his horse. He jumped at the sound of the horse's whinny in response to the intrusion, but sighed a breath of relief when he saw Marcos. "Oh, I was so deep in thought that you startled me," he said in a weak and very weary voice. "Did you succeed in getting Niccoli?"

"Yes, I have her well hidden," Marcos said sympathetically as he stepped up into the chariot. "Come, let us proceed with our plans."

He cracked the whip over the horses' heads and sped rapidly towards the bright sunlight of the open street. The chariot skidded around the corner, throwing dirt on everyone that was standing nearby. He was alert to any danger that might arise and scrutinized the movements of each person they passed. When they pulled up to the coliseum wall he quickly jumped down from the chariot and disappeared into the darkness of its corridor. Within minutes he returned with Niccoli.

Cornelius' eyes were fixed upon the bloodstained bundle that Marcos's held in his arms. As Marcos approached the chariot he stepped to the ground and slowly proceeded to meet him. He had not known what to expect and was fearful that there would have been nothing left of his daughter. Sobbing with relief to have Niccoli's body he fell to his knees in anguish. Blood stained his toga as he pressed Niccoli to his bosom in much the same manner as he had done so many years prior when he would soothe her scraped knees and hard bumps. "Niccoli, my Niccoli," he cried as he rocked her back and forth in a vain attempt to console both her and himself. Only another parent who had held their dead child in their arms could identify what he was feeling.

"I will help your fellow Christians," he whispered. "I will also seek out your God for whom you so courageously gave your life. I will learn more of this love your Jesus taught and I promise you, Niccoli, your death will not be in vain!"

Marcos stood aside to allow Cornelius his private time with his daughter and watched for anyone who might pose a threat to their safety. When he saw a soldier in the distance he gently nudged the senator, "Someone comes!" He warned. "Put Niccoli on the bed of the chariot and push her forward into the nose. Hide her as much as possible," he urged.

Cornelius reluctantly laid her down and tucked her into the front of the chariot. When he straightened up Marcos noticed blood on his toga and quickly arranged the folds of the toga to conceal the stain as best that he could. He clasped the hand of Cornelius to signify his friendship and devotion. Cornelius responded, and sealed the friendship by placing his hand on the shoulder of his companion and giving a nod of approval.

EPILOGUE

From her vantage point high above the coliseum arena Niccoli could see and hear the crowd of people but felt detached, as though she was only an observer. The feeling was like nothing she had ever felt before. Then she noticed a white mist rising from a mangled body on the arena floor. She blinked, not believing her eyes as she watched the white mist develop into the almost transparent form of Andrew. His entire countenance radiated with a glowing white essence and he beamed with joy as he greeted her.

"What is happening?" asked Niccoli. She was having trouble understanding what was occurring around her, everything seemed so strange. The wind was gently blowing and for the first time she looked down at the garment that was softly flapping against her body. The soft material was glistening white. "Where did this dress come from?" she questioned. "I remember no such dress."

"I think we have started a new life," replied Andrew.

They stood together and watched the same miracle happen to the remaining Christians. Soon they were all united once again and greeting one another in joyous reunion.

"So this is what death is all about?" remarked Niccoli. "It is nothing to be afraid of, but rather something to rejoice over!"

She had never felt such absolute peace and harmony as she did at this very moment, and love surrounded her as never before. She stood enraptured by the exquisite music that filled the heavens and, as the angelic figures drew closer, their harmonious notes filled the air with songs of love and praise.

Suddenly a bright light started to appear on the horizon. At first it appeared as a small flame, but its radiance gradually spread out in glowing rays that engulfed all the Christians in its brilliant light. The Roman coliseum faded from view and the blazing light started to take shape. Squinting their eyes against its brilliance, they soon were able to recognize the figure of Jesus welcoming them with outstretched arms.

Totally enthralled by the love and compassion that encompassed them, the Christians lifted their arms in humble adoration. The light pulsated in and around them as though it was in tune with the heartbeat of Jesus; captivating them and drawing them up like a magnet until every one was encased within the living arms of their Savior. In their wildest dreams they could never have imagined anything so beautiful. What a wondrous reward!

Niccoli's thoughts raced back to the words the Christians had spoken together shortly before entering the arena: "Surely goodness and mercy shall follow me all the days of my life. ***And I shall dwell in the house of the Lord forever***. Amen"

Niccoli's martyrdom was established from that fateful day forward. Not only for the love that she radiated while she lived, but for the bravery she displayed in her death. Word spread quickly of how she consoled her fellow prisoners during their captivity and had given them hope in their darkest hours.

Many spectators in the coliseum were moved by her display of courage as they watched her march forward leading the Christians with her head held high. They recalled how she had chanted 'Jesus, Jesus' exhibiting how proud she was to be a follower of Jesus.

In time Niccoli's body was moved to the garden of Agrippina where select Christians were enshrined. It was a place where all who so desired could come to acknowledge her bravery and love. She would be remembered and serve as an inspiration to those left behind who continued the ministry of her Lord.

It was because of Niccoli, and the many others who gave their lives teaching the love of Jesus, that the Christian movement grew and survived the atrocities inflicted by Nero. Niccoli's life displayed that even in the darkest hour God's love is there as a beacon for all who seek it.

THE LOVE OF GOD SURVIVES ALL! Situations and conflicts are 'Only Temporary' because He comforts and delivers us from all of our tribulations.

May we, like Niccoli, keep the faith and be a comfort to those who are in trouble, just as we are comforted by our Heavenly Father.

Printed in the United States
901900002B

9 781591 604174